WRIGHT KIND OF LOVE

WRIGHT KIND OF LOVE

WRIGHT DUET BOOK TWO

K.A. LINDE

PART I

UH-OH

HARLEY

My brothers were going to kill him.

I had not spent the last three years pining over Chase Sinclair for it to all go up in flames this fast. We'd sent an end date—graduation. Now that I had graduated and everything was finally falling into place, my brothers were trying to ruin it all.

It didn't matter that they'd shown up because they were concerned for me. My plan had always been law school. I was going to change the world. I'd even made a deal with the devil—my father, Owen Wright—to pay for the whole thing in exchange for his silence. Then, somehow, he'd found out that I'd withdrawn from Harvard Law and outed me to my four brothers.

Wrights and Sinclairs didn't mix.

Not after everything the Sinclairs had done to try to sabotage us.

And yet Chase and I worked.

We had from day one. But it had been our ten-year age gap, my nineteen years to his twenty-nine, that had scared him off more than anything my brothers would do. And now that I was a little older, I appreciated that he'd given me the time and space I needed to make my own decision.

And I'd chosen him.

I had chosen *him*.

So maybe it was me who was going to kill my brothers if they didn't back the fuck off.

"Stop!" I shouted.

Of course, no one stopped.

Chase was stuck in the doorframe of my bedroom with a bloody nose. Whitton and Julian held back Jordan as Weston fought to climb over the lot of them to get to Chase. They were like feral beasts. Fucking hell.

"I said, fucking stop!" I said, barreling into my brothers.

We were a fucked up lot. My twin brothers, Whitt and West, had grown up in Seattle, not knowing that we were the secret family to our father. Definitely not that he had another family, Jordan and Julian, across the border in Vancouver. It was the best part about all of us moving to Lubbock, Texas, where the Wright Construction head-quarters were. Now, we were a proper family.

Unfortunately, we were acting like a proper family.

All fucked up. All the time.

One of the benefits of having older brothers was that I could fight with the best of them. When I lowered my shoulder and popped them out of the way, Julian released an *oof*, and they shifted just enough for me to get through.

"I love her!" Chase shouted over the din of my brothers' rage. He straightened, dropping his hand that was now covered in blood. "I love her, all right?"

My heart stopped at those words. Those three little words. We hadn't used them earlier when we made our declaration. He had said that he was mine, that it had always been me, that I was his girlfriend. All things I'd wanted to hear for so long. But not the L-word.

I wasn't sure he'd even meant to say it here, but I couldn't keep the smile from breaking out on my face. He hadn't just claimed me in front of all of my brothers; he'd said he *loved* me. It was still unbelievable that those words had come out of his mouth. And to hear them as a declaration was indescribable.

When I reached him across the divide, he held his arm out, and I slid into the space against his chest. A unit. Together. Where we had always been apart. Now, it was us against the world. Just like I'd always wanted it to be.

"You don't even know her," Jordan argued.

"Love?" Whitt scoffed at the same time.

"The fuck?" West said.

Julian's jaw just dropped.

"Nothing you say is going to change how I feel," Chase said.

"And somehow, none of that is your business," I snapped.

"You have to be kidding me," Whitt began.

I cut him off. "I don't have to be doing anything. You all are absolutely out of fucking line. You came here because you were worried about me and devolved into *this*? You should be ashamed of yourselves."

My brothers looked among themselves. As if they

couldn't believe that I was going against them. As if, somehow, they'd thought I'd *want* them to punch Chase.

"He's just using you," Jordan added.

"He is *not* using me," I snapped.

"For the last time, Wright," Chase growled, "this has nothing to do with you."

"It is suspicious," Julian pointed out.

"It's not suspicious," I said, glaring at him.

He held his hands up and took a step back. "I was just saying," he muttered.

"Please, would everyone stop talking? Because I am so over every single thing about this already."

"Just explain what the fuck is going on," West said.

"I don't have to explain anything. In fact, you all should leave." I crossed my arms over my chest and narrowed my eyes at them. "Now."

"We're not leaving you alone with him," Jordan argued.

"Oh yes, you fucking are. You ruined my perfectly good evening. My graduation night at that. I could be out at the bars, screwing around, and none of you would care about that."

"I would," Whitt said, raising his hand.

"Shut it," I snarled. "And if you care about me being with Chase, then we can talk about it."

They all started to speak at once, but I held my hands up.

"But not now. Not when you're this riled up. Not when you're fucking *violent!*"

I shook my head. I had known it was going to be a disaster when I told my family what was going on. No one was going to be happy that I wasn't going to Harvard Law. They were going to try to talk me out of it. I'd been their hopes and dreams in that regard for far too long. And I'd known that after that talk, introducing Chase wasn't going to be fun.

I hadn't thought that Jordan would punch him.

He'd had his anger issues so closely under lock that I didn't even think he had that in him anymore. He'd tried so hard not to be like Owen. They all had. The fact that they didn't even see the trap they'd walked right into was sad. Owen had paved the way, and they'd fallen right for it. He'd barely had to spring the thing to get them all to do his dirty work for them.

I hoped they all felt fucking terrible when they realized it.

"So, get out." I pointed at the door.

"Harley," Whitt said, trying to reason with me with sympathy on his face.

"No."

"Come on," West said. "We'll be civil."

"You don't know what the word means."

"We should talk about this," Julian argued.

"No!" I snapped. "You all lost the opportunity to discuss this when you punched him in the face."

"You're just going to stand there and let her speak for you, Sinclair?" Jordan asked.

"She said everything that needs to be said," Chase said, tipping his head at my brother, his enemy.

I snapped my fingers at Jordan twice to get his eyes on me. "*She* is right in front of you. I speak for myself. Fuck off with the misogyny in my house." I strode across the living room and yanked the door open. "Now, get out."

My brothers looked torn between listening to me and continuing to have this out with Chase. I smacked my hand against the door.

"We will talk when you can be civil. That is not right now. So, go."

They grumbled, but to their credit, they slumped out the front door.

Jordan looked back at me once as he crossed back outside. "He's going to hurt you."

My face shuttered. "You don't know anything."

"I do. I know him."

"Maybe you *knew* him," I said. "But all I hear is that none of you trust me enough to make my own judgment call."

"None of us want to see you get hurt."

They were too late. Three years too late. Now, I was finally happy, and *they* were the ones ruining it.

"You can't save me from everything."

"We can try."

I shook my head at him and then shut the door in his face. I closed my eyes as I fought back the roiling emotions ripping through me. That had been an unmitigated disaster. I could not possibly think of a worse way for anyone to find out about us.

I didn't know where we went from here, but I knew that we couldn't keep going the way we had been. Everything had changed from this moment on.

Everything.

2

CHASE

"Well, that could have gone better."

Harley released a harsh laugh. "That's a word for it."

I cupped my still-bleeding nose. It fucking hurt. Jesus Christ, Jordan Wright had a mean right hook—I'd give him that. He certainly didn't miss.

Not that I'd anticipated him throwing that punch today. Sure, I was sleeping with his little sister. I'd known he would be pissed. That was why I'd hidden in her bedroom even though I fucking hated it. I hadn't wanted to hide like we'd hidden the last three years, and I'd done it when I saw the sheer panic cross her face at the sight of her brothers at the door.

I'd gotten a bloody nose out of the whole mess.

Maybe not undeserved, but still...fuck him.

"Are you okay?" I asked as I headed across the living room to Harley.

Her eyes slid to mine, and then she frowned. "Am *I* okay? Jesus, Chase, you're still bleeding."

She rushed into the kitchen and returned a moment later with a towel, which she held up to my face. My hands had blood on them. It had run like rivulets down my forearms. It was red and tacky, running down my lip and on my chin. It was probably on my shirt.

I liked this shirt. Fuck.

I winced when the towel touched my nose. "Well, fuck. Don't think I'm going to escape another Wright black eye."

"My fucking brothers," she growled.

"I'd say it was just Jordan, but West did swing on me. I just saw that one coming."

She huffed. "I can't believe them."

"Can't you?"

"Well, yes. That wasn't how I wanted them to find out," she said. "But still..."

"Still," I agreed.

"Come on. Let me get you some ice."

She drew me into the kitchen and rummaged through a drawer to pull out a plastic baggie. She opened the freezer and dumped cubes into the bag, wrapped it in another kitchen towel, and then brought it to me.

"Here." She took the bloodied towel she had first given to me and then gently replaced it with the ice.

I cringed as it touched my nose.

"Does it hurt?" she asked, pulling back.

But I reached for her wrist and guided the ice back onto my nose. "It's already feeling better."

Her answering smile made all the pain disappear. "You poor thing. I'm going to have to take real good care of you."

She tipped up onto her toes and drew my mouth down to hers. I jerked back in surprise at the cool temperature. She gave me a sly smirk.

"Yes?" she asked.

I had no words as she slipped a piece of ice across her tongue. Blood pumped in completely different places than from my recent injury. She was pure temptation in that moment. And yet it felt like a distraction.

"Should we talk about what happened?"

"I don't want to talk. I want to make you feel better. Kiss away your pain."

I shot her an exasperated expression. "Don't think you can kiss away my black eye."

Light twinkled in her eye. "Oh, I wasn't planning to kiss you *there*."

Her lips pressed against my throat. Cold ice slithered down the exposed column, and the shock of different temperatures made my cock swell with desire. My hands came to her hips, dragging her harder against me.

"Harley..." I ground out.

She responded by opening the buttons of my now-bloodied shirt. "Think we should get you out of this. It might need to be washed."

I huffed out a laugh. Then, her cold tongue was on my chest, working a trail of hot and cold along my exposed abdomen and lower, lower, lower.

"You're not going to get out of talking to me about this," I told her.

"Okay," she said, coming back to her feet. "Let's talk."

"Really?" I asked in surprise.

Her big blue eyes were lined in silver, and her smile

was magnetic as she leaned against me. "So...you love me?"

"I do." My voice was low and earnest. "Not how I planned to tell you that either."

"But you love me."

"Yes."

"Say it again," she whispered.

"I love you."

She shivered at the words. "How long have you known?"

I drew her against me, my heart cracking open for her. "I've always known."

"Always?"

I nodded. "Always with you, baby girl."

"That's convenient," she said softly.

"Oh?"

"Because I love you, too."

She threw her arms around my neck and pressed her lips to mine. I took everything she was offering. Forget talking about her brothers and that catastrophe and my bloody nose. All that mattered was that my girl was in my arms and she'd said the words I'd always wanted to hear from her. The words I'd always wanted to give to her.

The ice was still in her mouth when our lips touched. Her tongue was cold as I opened her lips and brushed mine, warm, against hers. She sighed against me and passed the shrinking ice cube to me. I took it from her, heating up her cold mouth with mine.

"Oh," she gasped as my hands slipped under the edges of her tank top and ran under her breasts.

I kept going north until I cupped her breast in my

hand, rolling her nipple between my fingers. She writhed against me. Her hips rolling in a familiar motion that said she was heating up, just like I was. I teased the other pert nipple between my fingers until she pulled back from my kiss with hazy desire in her eyes.

"Fuck," she managed.

My hands slid down her sides and cupped her ass. I lifted her up, aligning our bodies so my cock nestled against the heat of her pussy. She draped her legs around my hips, rocking herself against me to try to find that perfect friction.

I carried her out of the kitchen and into the living room, where I hastily pushed everything off of the coffee table, throwing the contents onto the floor. Then, I lowered her ass onto the edge of the wooden table. Her back hit next as I pushed her down flat. Her blue eyes were round with desire as I stripped her shorts off and let her thong follow into a discarded pile behind me.

The ice was fast melting in my mouth, but I had enough left to tease her the way she had been teasing me.

I spread her legs wide. One hand holding her open for my perusal, the other sliding up the slick seam of her pussy. She shuddered under my touch. A soft gasp leaving her lips.

"So wet for me, baby girl."

"Yes," she whimpered when I pulled my fingers away.

My mouth moved to her inner thigh. My tongue flicked against the skin before I replaced it with the ice cube. She bucked on the table as I dragged the cold cube down her inner thigh with my teeth. I stopped right before I knew she wanted me and didn't miss the little rise of her hips, as if she could force me to keep going.

I chuckled softly and moved to the other leg, using the ice all the way down. She gasped when I slipped it just barely against her waiting pussy lips before pulling it back into my mouth.

"So fucking sweet."

"Fuck, Chase."

"Too cold?" I teased.

"Too everything."

And I knew she meant it. Her chest was rising and falling rapidly. Her eyes were squeezed shut. Her hands clenched on the edge of the table. As if she could barely breathe with anticipation.

"Hey, eyes on me."

She slowly obliged, meeting my gaze.

"Up on your elbows."

She swallowed and then lifted her torso up. "Like this?"

"I want you to watch me eat your cunt."

Her jaw dropped and legs quivered at the filthy words. I popped the remains of the ice cube out of my mouth, slicked it once through her wet pussy, and then carefully slid it into her mouth, where it would quickly dissolve.

"Now, you see how good you taste."

Her tongue swirled around the ice cube, making me think about the incredible way she used it on my cock. We'd have time for that later. Then, I lowered my head and devoured her. My eyes slipped up to hers to make sure she watched as my tongue flicked against the sensitive ball of nerves at the apex of her thighs. If she was watching my fingers sink inches deep in and out of her. If she was imagining my cock fucking her in the same manner.

Her face was a tableau of desire mapped on every surface. She coiled and coiled and coiled up as if she were preparing to explode from watching me eating her out.

So, I gave her everything she wanted, and she watched like that coiled viper as I did it. Until she was trembling under my touch. Little mewling whimpers escaping her mouth. Until everything tightened under my touch and she exploded.

She dropped back off of her elbows and arched as the climax hit her. I continued circling her clit as I watched her come undone in all of its magnificence.

When she was finished, she barely took a breath before launching herself at me. I coughed out a laugh as she tackled me backward onto the floor. She made quick work of my pants, shucking them to the floor. My cock sprang free from its restraints, thick and long, rigid with my need for her. She straddled my hips in one swift motion and poised her now-primed opening above my aching cock.

Her eyes were half-lidded as she looked down upon me over the bridge of her nose. "Make me do that again."

Her wish. My command.

I gripped her hips in my hands and slammed her down onto me. We both groaned at the same time. Me stretching her wide open. The feel of her silken heat around me. Wet and warm and pulsing still from the remnants of her last orgasm.

"Fuck me," I groaned.

"Oh, I plan to."

Then, she rolled her hips in a way that sent pleasure straight through me.

"Uh-uh," she teased. She pointed two fingers from my eyes to hers as she rode me. "Look right here."

I growled in the back of my throat as I came up to my elbows to watch her work her pussy on me.

"Is that better?" I asked, my eyes fixed on the place where we came apart and snapped back together.

"Oh yes," she breathed. "That angle…"

I met her next downward thrust with an upward one of my own. "*That* angle?"

She cried out at the feel of me getting deeper in her. "Yes. Deeper."

"Harder?" I countered.

"And faster."

I pushed fully to sitting until she was in my lap and bounced her relentlessly up and down. There was less room to maneuver, but every hip movement hit that much harder. Until we both were panting from exertion and so very close to the edge.

"Come with me," I told her.

She gripped on to me harder as we both unleashed together. I grunted into her shoulder, pistoning my cock deeper as I came hard and fast.

She trailed kisses along my shoulder when she finally settled from the orgasm. I still hadn't let her go.

"God," she murmured. "If this is how you say I love you…"

I laughed softly. "I do love you."

"Good." She pulled back and looked at me. "Because you're definitely going to have a black eye."

"I know. It was worth it."

"Was it?" she asked, biting her lip.

"I'm not hiding anymore, Harley. We spent too long lurking in the shadows of each other's lives. I want daylight with you. I want all the things we never had, and no one and nothing is going to keep you from me—do you understand? If I have to face down the whole town to make you mine, then so be it."

She flushed all over, a smile finally gracing her features. "Then so be it."

3

HARLEY

Chase stayed the night.

He was still here the next morning when Bailey came home and commented on the state of the living room, proclaiming immediately that she just didn't want to know what had happened. Though, at the worsening look of Chase's black eye, she was curious.

"So, your brothers flipped? I knew Whitt would," Bailey said. "Eve and I can talk him down. Should I make the call?"

I shook my head. "I appreciate it, but it's not your fight."

"It shouldn't be a fight at all," Bailey said.

"I agree, but I probably need to sit down and have a real conversation with them."

"How about this? *We're together. Fuck off.* Does that work?"

"I agree with Bailey," Chase said. He stepped out of my bedroom, running a towel through his hair.

It still mystified me to have him in my house. Like in

the house I rented and not at the house he owned. It was such a big step even though every other one we'd made recently should seem more significant. This one hit me the hardest.

I'd always belonged in his world, and he'd never belonged in mine.

Until now.

So seeing him with wet hair, using my cheap towel and smelling like my floral shampoo, was a whole new experience. And I liked it.

"Well, there will be no conversation about whether we're dating. That's decided. But I did want to bring them in on this easier. They're my family. I want to smooth it over."

"I still think I should go with you," Chase said.

"She said smooth it over," Bailey pointed out. "I doubt you'd do much more than make it worse."

"She's right."

"I liked it better when she was on my side," Chase argued.

"Too late, lover boy. I'm always on Harley's," Bailey countered. "You're just lucky you're on her side."

"I am, aren't I?" Then, he stepped forward and kissed me long and hard. "So very lucky."

Bailey sighed dramatically. "I'm going to have to deal with PDA all the time, aren't I?"

"Probably," I said with a laugh.

"Definitely," Chase said.

Even that small word made me swoon. We were a couple. The thing I'd wanted for three years that I was sure would never happen was now my reality. And every time I looked up at him and remembered he was mine, something fluttered in my chest all over again.

"I should probably go deal with my brothers though."

He sighed. "If you're sure."

"I am. We need to have this out. This isn't going to be the last time they see us together. And they're going to have to get used to the idea."

"Doubtful," Bailey muttered under her breath.

I shot her a look, and she barely muffled her laughter. "Keep it together, Bails."

"I love you, Harley Davidson," she said with a head-shake. "But your brothers are over-the-top protective. I get it; Eve is that way with me. But *four* brothers? That's a lot." Her eyes flickered to Chase. "Better be ready for the fallout."

"I'm ready," he said easily.

"There will be no fallout. There will only be them getting used to the idea and dealing with it."

"If you'd thought that was true, then you would have told them about this," she said, pointing between us, "a long time ago."

She was right. I hated that she was right.

I huffed out a breath. "Well, might as well at least deal with damage control."

Chase pressed a kiss to my forehead. "You'll be fine. I have faith in you."

"Yeah. I also have an ace in my pocket."

Bailey raised an eyebrow.

"Mom is here."

She laughed. "Lord help those boys."

My mom was staying at Whitt's house for the week. I was proud that I'd gotten her to agree to come for a whole week. She hadn't been to Lubbock for more than moving me out and back in since I'd moved here. Not with Grandma and Grandpa to look after. I was going to be sad when she left again tomorrow afternoon, but I was glad to have her here today.

She pulled me into a hug when I walked into my brother's house. "Hey, sweetheart."

I breathed in her familiar scent. "Hey, Mom."

"I heard about what happened."

"Whitt told you?"

"He did. I didn't realize until it was too late that all your brothers had disappeared last night. I'm so sorry that happened to you." She touched my cheek. "You didn't deserve that."

Tears came to my eyes at her words. God, I hadn't realized how much I just wanted someone to take away all my problems until that moment. How much easier it would be to just sic Mom on them and make it all stop. But I couldn't do that, unfortunately.

"Thanks, Mom. It wasn't fun—that's for sure."

"And Chase?" she asked.

"Fine."

She arched an eyebrow. "Not the way I heard it."

"Well, he has a black eye."

She sighed heavily. "I'm really sorry, sweetie. I sent you after him because I wanted you to have your moment alone. Not to get bombarded by your brothers.

If it's any consolation, Eve really went after Whitt about it last night."

I laughed. "Oh man, I wish I could have seen that."

"I know you don't want to hear this with everything else, but you should really call your father."

I froze at those words. Call my father. Owen fucking Wright. The man who had manipulated me into going to the law school he wanted. Who had thrown a tantrum the second he found out I hadn't done what he wanted. Who constantly ruined everyone's life he touched.

"No." The word left my mouth before I could think.

"Honey."

"No," I said more firmly. "Absolutely fucking not. He is the reason that all of this happened in the first place."

My mom sighed softly. "You could have told your brothers about your relationship. They didn't have to find out the way that they did."

She was right. I could have told them at any time. And they would have reacted the same way. But the fact that Owen had done this on purpose was inexcusable. Not to mention that when he'd found out the information, his first instinct had been how to use it against me. I owed him nothing. Not ever again.

"Will you ever see the worst in him, Mom?" I asked instead of the torrent of anger that foamed at my mouth.

"Will you ever see the best?"

"No," I told her. "I don't see anything good in him."

"He's your father."

"He might as well not be for all that he did to raise me. You were there every day, Mom. Whitt and West were around. Even Grandma and Grandpa were around. Owen might as well just be a sperm donor."

My mom winced at those words. I hadn't meant to hurt her, but God, it was the truth. Why was she the only one who didn't see it?

"I suppose it's easy to see it that way from your perspective," she said softly.

"I'm sorry, Mom. I know you loved him, but even you have to admit that he used you and hurt our family. He was never what you deserved."

"What's going on over here?" Whitt asked as he strode out of his bedroom. My brother was, of course, in a black suit with a blue tie knotted tight at his throat. He didn't even have work today. He just couldn't help himself.

"Just talking," Mom said, backing away from the painful conversation she never wanted to have. Easier to look at anything but in the mirror.

Whitt looked me over with a sigh. "How are you this morning, Harley?"

"Been better," I told him. "Heard your night wasn't as great as you'd imagined either."

"Considering I'd thought I was going to be spending the night with my fiancée and not relegated to the couch," he muttered under his breath.

Fiancée. Gah, as mad as I was at him, I loved that he'd proposed yesterday. That Eve was going to be my sister soon. That made Bailey a sister in truth, too.

"Eve sent you to the couch in your own house?"

"I sure did," Eve said. She was in a knee-length green dress and her signature black leather Louboutin heels.

Her dark hair was long down her back in supermodel waves. "Well, for part of the night."

Whitt shot her a look of abject devotion. "It was fair. Yesterday was...a lot."

"Is that an apology?" I asked.

Whitt said nothing. Eve cleared her throat noisily.

"Were you expecting one?" he asked.

I huffed. "You're ridiculous. I texted West, Jordan, and Julian, and they're on their way over to talk about this."

"We have brunch plans," he said, gesturing to their attire.

Eve rolled her eyes. "Canceled plans. You need to *fix* this, Whitton."

Oh, pulling out his whole name.

He sighed, as if already knowing that he'd lost. "Fine. Let's talk."

Eve smirked and stepped toward me, pulling me into a hug. "Before you get in with the guys, just know that I'm so fucking happy for you."

"Thanks, Eve."

She pulled back but kept her hands on my shoulders. "Seriously, Chase Sinclair is a good guy. None of you are like your dad, and he isn't like his. We shouldn't judge him based off of his entire family if y'all don't want to be judged off of your bad apple."

The words were directed at me, but I could feel Whitt tense across the room. We weren't Owen. Chase wasn't Arnold. And Eve would know. She'd dated Chase's dad after all. She knew the depths of his treachery and had come out on top anyway. I appreciated her saying it.

A knock at the door pulled us apart. Whitt yanked it

open to find Jordan and Julian standing at the threshold. Both men were in a suit and looked like they were going to be heading to church at any second. West was jogging up the drive in ripped jeans and a band shirt. He was definitely not heading to church. He had to leave in the afternoon to get back on the road with his band, Cosmere. They were touring for another month. Right up until West's wedding with Nora.

"Come on in," Whitt said with a sigh.

Mom stepped forward, hugging all the boys and welcoming them inside. Then, with a pointed look, she took her soon-to-be daughter-in-law to another room. I knew they'd be there for backup if I needed them, but the guilty looks on my brothers' faces told me I wasn't going to need it.

"Have you all calmed down?" I asked.

"Anyone else get in trouble with their significant other last night?" Whitt grumbled, dropping into a chair across from his twin.

West, Jordan, and Julian all slowly raised their hands. I couldn't help it; I laughed.

"Perhaps Nora, Annie, and Jennifer also reminded you that you all grossly overreacted, as Eve did to Whitt."

"We were just looking out for you," Julian said.

"Looking out for me by punching Chase in the face?"

Julian threw a thumb at Jordan. "He did that."

Jordan arched an eyebrow. "Throw me under the bus, why don't you?"

"I threw a punch, too," West said with a shrug. "And honestly, he had it coming."

The other guys leaned forward in agreement.

I held up a hand. "I actually didn't call you here to discuss Chase. So, I don't want this to devolve into your opinions on our relationship. We're in a relationship. I've been into him since *your* wedding," I said, pointing at Jordan.

Jordan's jaw clenched. "That was three years ago."

"Well aware," I said with a shrug. "Why do you think I didn't tell you?"

"Because you were a teenager!" Whitt snapped.

"Chase did the *right thing* by not pursuing me then because he knew I was too young."

"You're still too young," Jordan muttered under his breath.

"Anyway, that doesn't matter. I'm old enough to see that he made the right call and to know that I want to be with him. I didn't drop Harvard because of him. I did it because I wanted to take the job at Wright Construction. We already talked about that. That *was* my dream, but it isn't any longer. I really want to do this, and I have no ulterior motive." They looked skeptical, so I barreled forward anyway. "The real problem is Owen."

Jordan tensed. He'd been the one to answer the phone when he called. He'd been the one to give in. He had to feel like a dupe.

"He played us," Jordan inferred.

"Yep. All of us. Me included." I sighed. "Because I didn't just agree to go to Harvard Law if I got in. I did it in exchange for his silence about Chase."

Julian blinked hard at me. "What?"

"Are you nuts?" West asked.

Whitt ground his teeth together. "Harley."

But it was Jordan who was silent the longest before exhaling. "Ah, that makes more sense."

"Does it?"

"He would use it as leverage to get back with you. I couldn't figure it out before. Why you'd let him back in when you were the one who hated him the most."

"I didn't want to."

"You feared our reaction enough that you'd work with him before telling us," Jordan inferred.

I bit my lip and nodded. "I mean, that's the gist of it."

"I'm sorry," he said softly. "I'm sorry we made you feel that way. That you had to deal with him without us. And that we proved you right."

My heart clenched at those words. The apology that I deserved. Even if it was only in my father's duplicity that I had gotten it. Jordan might still hate that we were together, but there was someone we all hated more —Owen.

"I don't want this to come between us. I don't want this to make Owen win. I don't want him to win in anything. He's hurt us all too much, and he did this, knowing it would drive a wedge between us. He used this to get back into your good graces, and frankly, he doesn't deserve it. He never has. And I regret not just telling you so that I wouldn't have entered into that stupid agreement."

"Blocking him was the best decision I've made," Whitt said.

West pulled out his phone. "I'll do it, too."

Julian wavered and then took out his phone. "If he'd do it to Harley, he'd do it to any of us."

Jordan came to his feet and pulled me into a hug. "I don't like this. I hate Chase Sinclair. But I love you, okay?"

I laughed. "Okay."

Whitt sighed. "His family is scum. But I won't patronize you and act like you haven't thought about it."

"I have."

West ruffled my hair. "It's weird to think of you with anyone."

"It's almost like you've all run off any possible guys."

Julian laughed. "Then, we're doing our job."

I rolled my eyes.

"Look," Jordan said, "I'll be cool about this for now. But if he hurts you, I'll kill him."

My other brothers nodded in agreement. And I just laughed.

"I can live with that."

4

CHASE

"Do I want to know why you have a black eye?" Kai asked when I showed up at my house.

"You really don't." I sighed and bent down to ruffle Bowie's fur. My ridiculous, horribly trained golden retriever was all energy and wet kisses. "Hey, bud. I know. I'm sorry I was gone all night. Next time, I'll bring you with me."

"And why you have blood on your shirt."

I glanced down at the material. I really did like this shirt. Damn.

"Ran into someone's fist."

"On purpose?" Kai asked with a laugh.

"Not exactly."

I'd known Kai Cruz for years. We'd hit it off together at UT Austin Law and gotten jobs at the same law firm in Houston. When we decided to both move back to Lubbock, I was glad that we were opening the firm together. That his wife, Elsie, was from Clovis, New Mexico, and that they both wanted to make the trip. I hadn't thought that I'd leave the firm to start working for my father until I actually did it. The fact that Kai didn't hate me for it made him an even better person.

"This about your girl?" he surmised.

"Harley," I filled him in.

"Yeah, Elsie mentioned her from the concert."

I might have confessed my interest in her to Elsie when I was drunk that night. Whoops.

"I figured she might tell you."

"Elsie tells me everything. So, when do we get to officially meet her?"

"Whenever you want." I held my hand out. "Thanks for watching Bowie."

"The dog is cooler than you," he said as he took my hand.

I laughed. "That's fair."

"I'm serious. If I tell Elsie, she's going to start hounding you."

"Tell her to pick the day and time."

Kai nodded, satisfied. "Done. You should put ice on this."

I swatted him away. "Yeah, yeah."

Kai left with a chuckle. I fed Bowie, changed into gym clothes, and took the dog for a good, long walk. He needed it after a night without me. I always felt guilty leaving Bowie behind. I'd known that Harley wouldn't mind, but I'd wanted it to just be us.

When I made it back to the house, a car was parked in the driveway. A car that I recognized.

"Oh boy," I muttered under my breath.

Annie stepped out of the driver's side as I walked up

to her. Her red hair was down in loose waves. She wore typical Annie attire—short shorts, a tank top, and cowboy boots. I let Bowie loose, and he all but tackled her to the ground with kisses. She laughed and played with him as I strolled up to them.

"Annie," I said in greeting.

She glanced up at me and shook her head. "Look at you."

"I assume Jordan told you."

"You assume right," she said as she rose to her feet.

She reached forward and put her fingers on my swollen nose. I hissed between my teeth and jerked back.

"That bastard," she said, though it sounded almost affectionate. "I cannot believe he punched you. Again!"

"Yeah. It wasn't exactly how I wanted to end my day either." I gestured to the door. "Come in?"

Annie and I had had our ups and downs over the years. When we'd been in high school, we'd been an item. Then, when I went away to Yale, we made a pact to get married if we weren't married before we were thirty. She'd married Jordan right before that mark. I'd thought for a long time that we'd work out, but now, I saw how ridiculous that had been.

It had taken someone like Harley to show me how wrong Annie and I really were for each other. She was my best friend. The person who had been there for me. But Harley was the person who completed me. And it wasn't even a contest. I just hadn't known until I'd met the other half of my heart.

Annie stopped at the kitchen island, and when I reached her, she punched my shoulder.

"Ouch!" I cried. "What the fuck, Annie?"

"That's for hiding this from me, you idiot!"

I laughed and rubbed my arm. "Did you have to hit me? I've had enough of that for one day."

"Well, Jordan was out of line, but I'm allowed to be mad that you didn't feel you could tell me."

"It's not about you."

"No," she said easily, slipping onto the island barstool. "You thought I'd tell Jordan."

"Wouldn't you?"

She bit her lip. "I don't know. Guess we'll never know."

"To be fair, we weren't official until yesterday."

"That is not fair because you told Jordan that you're in love with her." Annie's eyes rounded. "You love her?"

"I do," I told her.

"When did it start?"

I rubbed the back of my head and glanced uneasily up at her. "At your wedding."

She coughed around a gasp. "Chase Sinclair! That was three years ago."

"I know."

"She was nineteen!"

"I actually didn't know that until after," I told her, as if that made it okay. "I'd been avoiding Wrights since you and Jordan..."

"Yeah. But, damn..."

"When I found out, I broke it off and told her that it couldn't happen."

"And yet you're together now."

I nodded. "We kept being in each other's orbit, and

she's my person, Annie. I waited until graduation, but I wasn't going to wait another day longer."

"She's a lucky woman," Annie told me fondly.

"Nah, I'm the lucky one."

Annie sighed. "Well, I suppose if you're going to get punched for something, it might as well be love."

"I actually think it's because I'm sleeping with Jordan's little sister and he hates me."

She shot me a disgruntled look. "Thanks for that visual."

I laughed and nudged her. "Hey, you're with Jordan. I never want to think about *that* either."

"Fair. So...where is Harley now?"

"Dealing with her brothers," I said on a wince. "I wanted to go with her, but she insisted that she do it alone."

"She can handle them. Give her some credit."

"I give her all the credit," I countered. "I just don't want her to have to deal with them by herself."

"My little romantic," Annie said with a smile.

"You're not mad?"

I didn't know why I'd asked it. It didn't matter what Annie thought about my relationship any more than what Harley's brothers thought about the situation. It wasn't going to change anything between us. I loved her. She was mine.

And yet...I wanted her approval. She was *Annie*. We'd been friends too long to not want things to be good between us.

"Mad that you didn't tell me? Yes. Mad about you and Harley? Of course not. I love Harley. She's one of the coolest people I've ever met." She pursed her lips and looked me up and down. "Actually, now that I think about it, you two make a lot of sense. The same family thing with your dads and your love of Halloween, and you listen to the same music." Her eyes skipped to my immense record collection.

She'd never understood my obsession with classic rock music. She always went for country or pop. Harley and I loved all the same things.

"She's strong. She's smart. She's funny. I bet she keeps you on your toes."

I smirked. "She does."

"Good. You need someone to challenge you. Anything too easy, and you're bored. You've always been that way."

"Thanks?" I said it more as a question.

"You're welcome, ass," she said with a laugh. "You need to be intellectually stimulated. You need constant competition. You need lots of interests. You're nonstop all the time. You've never slowed down a day in your life. Anyone who can keep up—or even better yet, make you put in the work—is going to be good for you."

"You've thought a lot about this."

She shrugged. "I had a lot of reason to."

Her smile was sincere and joyful, not tinged with sadness, as it had been for so long.

Annie had so many of those qualities that she had described. Still, we weren't the match. Jordan, as much as I hated him, had proven himself time and again to be hers. Harley just happened to be mine.

"She's the one," I told her.

"I'm so glad."

She pulled me in for a hug. My best friend. My longest friend. The person who understood me better than almost anyone. I'd put distance between us for so long because of our stupid pact and Jordan. It was nice to have her back. Back and better than ever because none of the tension remained. Just a strong friendship.

I released her, and she settled back onto her barstool. Then, I went to the kitchen and began making us breakfast. She was a French toast fan, and I remembered just how she liked them.

We were almost finished eating when the door opened, and Harley Wright stepped inside. She stopped for a second in the doorway, looking between us in confusion.

I'd given her a key last night.

I loved that she'd felt comfortable enough to use it.

A smile broke out on my face, but it was Annie who jumped up first. She stalked across the room and threw her arms around my girlfriend.

"Gah, I'm so fucking happy for you."

Harley looked at me over Annie's shoulder. Surprise was written into every line of her face. Then, she slowly put her arms around her sister-in-law and patted her twice.

"Hey, Annie. Didn't know you'd be here."

"Had to come and get the details from your boyfriend."

Her smile went from wary to satisfied in the blink of an eye. The first person to call me her boyfriend to her face, and oh, I could see she liked that.

"And what did he tell you?"

"That you were *nineteen* when you first hooked up at my wedding, and the jerk never told me anything." Annie stuck her tongue out at me.

"That's true. We weren't exactly advertising our non-relationship."

"Well, advertise it now because if the way he talks about you is how it usually is, then it's fucking adorable."

Harley grinned. Her gaze met mine again, and I saw questions in the lines of her shoulders. As if she was wondering what exactly I'd said. I'd be happy to tell her everything.

Annie must have read the room because she hugged Harley one more time. "He's all yours. I'm going to go make up with my husband."

"Don't make that sound so sexual," I called after her.

She flipped me off, and I could almost ignore her whispering, "Makeup sex," to Harley.

Somehow, I restrained my gag.

Harley just laughed. Then, she was running across the room, throwing her arms around me. My lips were on hers, and she was against me, and the entire world was right, as it was supposed to be.

"She said you're my boyfriend," she said against my lips.

"I am, baby girl."

"Never going to get used to hearing it."

"Oh, you are. I'm going to say it so much that you're going to tell me to stop."

"Am not."

I laughed. "Your boyfriend thinks that we should go kayaking."

Her eyes lit up. "This feels familiar."

"Thought we could have the date we never got to have all those years ago."

Harley had come over after the first time we'd been together so that we could go kayaking. But my sister, Ashleigh, informed me of Harley's nineteen years, and I had to cancel everything. We'd never gotten that date. And I wanted to make that right.

"What do you think?"

"Your girlfriend thinks yes."

Then, I kissed her again, tasting the word *girlfriend* on her tongue.

5
———

HARLEY

"I am no good at this," I said as I worked my paddle.

"You're going to get it. I've been doing it for years."

I turned around to look at him in the back of the two-person kayak. I was sure he was patronizing me, but he was sincere.

I wanted to be good at everything all the time. Sometimes, it was even hard to start new things because I wasn't automatically good. Paralysis from the fear of failure. But Chase was coaxing me into trying something new even if I was bad. He was probably good enough for both of us after all anyway.

He had individual kayaks as well, but I was glad we'd chosen the double because he could maneuver us when I got tired. I still ice-skated at the small rink that belonged to Tech, but that really didn't require arm strength. Totally different dynamics.

"Like this?" I asked, pushing hard into the water.

"Like that," he encouraged.

We were going just fine. I was finally getting the hang of it. We were moving across the water. Out in the middle of this beautiful lake, and I was seeing it from a totally different perspective. The canyon walls up high all around us. Bowie barking from the shoreline. Other people enjoyed their lake day far off in the distance. Just blurs on the horizon.

I was so focused on what was ahead of me that I didn't look where we were going.

"Harley!" Chase said as I dipped my oar too close to the floating deck.

"Shit!" I cried.

Everything happened in slow motion. I lost my balance. My body tilted sideways. A gasp escaped my mouth. And then we were tipping. Chase tried to keep us upright, but even he couldn't completely counter my full body weight. Suddenly, gravity took over and dumped us unceremoniously into the water.

I came up sputtering, my oar a dozen feet away in the opposite direction of the kayak.

Chase's head breached the surface of the water. He looked around in exasperation at the mess I'd caused. And then he burst into laughter.

Our eyes met, and I started laughing, too.

"Oops," I managed.

"I used to tip over a lot more," he said. He shook out his wet hair. "I forgot about that."

He swam toward the kayak. I went after my loose oar, and after a few minutes, we had the equipment.

"Come on. Swim to the deck."

I followed him with my one oar in my hand as he

navigated the kayak back toward the floating deck that I'd careened us into. I dropped the oar onto the deck and used the ladder to hoist myself up onto its surface. The sun was beating down on the wooden slats, and it felt good against my now-chilled skin to pass out, panting against it.

Chase secured the kayak, dropping both oars back into the boat before pulling himself up. My eyes dragged down his sculpted body. The hours on the water and in the gym sure had chiseled his arms and chest, and the defined V that led down to the now-soaked board shorts that clung to every inch of his powerful thighs and stirring cock. My mouth went dry.

"Well, hello," I murmured.

His eyes skimmed every inch of me spread before him on the deck in nothing but my tiny black bikini.

I crooked my finger at him. He smirked and dropped down beside me. His lips kissed the water-soaked skin of my stomach, his hands running over my breasts, our bodies aligning. I moaned as he brought his tongue to the sensitive skin at my throat. I arched against him to give him better access as I clutched on to his muscled shoulders.

"Someone could see," he warned.

"Someone could have seen in the parking garage in Seattle." I reminded him of that time we'd been so feverish for each other that we fucked right then and there.

His pupils dilated at the memory. "I had to have you then."

"And now?"

He responded by tugging on the string of my bikini top, exposing my breasts to the elements.

He dipped his head down, drawing a nipple into his mouth, swirling his tongue around the pebbled flesh. I shivered against him. My body ached for him in all the best places. I reached for his shorts, running a finger along the top of the bottoms. He thrust his hips hard against me, and I could feel the hard length of him through the heavy material.

"Need you out of these," I gasped.

"And this," he agreed as he plucked at the string of my bottoms. "Fuck."

I pushed at his shorts, but his eyes were transfixed on my lower half.

"Chase," I pleaded.

"Look at this pretty pink pussy," he said as he drew his fingers through the slick folds.

I groaned, holding on to his shorts for dear life at the sheer torture of him. He slipped his fingers up and circled the sensitive ball of nerves.

"Never want to get the taste of you out of my mouth."

Then, he dropped down to put his face between my legs. He dragged his tongue up the seam, pushing against my clit at the apex. I shuddered under his touch, and he did it again, as if I was the most delicious thing he'd ever tasted.

"Chase Sinclair," I ground out.

"Hmm?" he asked. His eyes were on me as he flicked his tongue against me again.

"Fuck me right this minute."

"Well, if you insist."

"I fucking insist."

He chuckled under his breath and then shucked his shorts to the deck floor. He settled between my thighs, brushing a stray wet strand of my blonde hair off my face. Our blue eyes met and locked, like someone had turned a key.

When he slid inside, I held that eye contact, even as everything in me said to close my eyes because, fuck, he felt incredible. But I kept that gaze and let him see my pleasure like a window to my very soul. Because I was bare for him in every way. This was it for me.

"You feel so good," he huffed on a breath as he pulled out and pushed back in until he was buried to the hilt. "Like you were made for me."

"Yes," I whispered.

"Want to be doing this every day."

Another hard thrust in.

"Please."

He started up a rhythm, and our bodies smacked noisily across the quiet lake. We were secluded enough that I was pretty sure that no one else could hear, but I wasn't sure I cared if someone did. The moment was punctuated with intense longing and gasped breaths as we came apart and together over and over again.

His hand came to my hip, using it as leverage to get even deeper. And it was this new depth that sent me shattering over the edge.

"Chase," I gasped as I dropped out of my body.

He was still going, milking my orgasm to draw out his own. When he came, it was hard and fast. He tipped his head back, a roar leaving his mouth as it took him.

I pressed my hand to his cheek when he came back to me. Then, I dragged his lips to mine. "Love to watch that."

He nipped at my bottom lip. "I'll give you as many as you want."

"All of them."

He slid out of me, returning his shorts and rolling over next to me. I righted my bikini. He drew me against him, sliding his arm under my shoulders. The world continued on around us, but there was just me and him here in this moment.

"Let's stay here forever," I whispered against his chest.

"Deal."

We stayed there on the deck in silence with him running his fingers through the wet strands of my hair. Only our heartbeats and the outdoor symphony our peaceful music.

Then, Chase came up to an elbow, leaning over my now-dry body, and pressed a kiss to my lips. "There's another thing we have to figure out."

"Oh?"

"My family."

I wrinkled my nose. "Do we have to tell them?"

He laughed. "I thought you'd be hounding me to do just that."

"Well, I mean, I want people to know."

"Exactly."

"But family is complicated."

He brushed his nose against mine. "Yeah, well, if you had to deal with all of your brothers at once, I should be able to figure out how to tell my family." He pursed his lips. "Gradually."

I laughed. "You mean, you don't want them to walk in on us?"

"It was efficient, I suppose." I touched the black under his eye, and he winced. "Though maybe a little more painful physically than I'd planned."

"At least no one is going to punch you in your family."

His eyes went distant. "Hmm…"

"Chase!" I said with a laugh. "Stop! No one is going to punch you."

"No, but…well, my dad is going to be a problem."

"Yeah. Our dads suck. What else is new?"

"We should tell my mom first."

I nodded. "That's fine. We don't have to do it all at once. We can take it slow. I don't care, Chase. I just care that you're mine. You're mine, right?"

"I'm yours."

"Good."

"I'm not doing this in half measures, Harley. Everyone is going to know that you're mine. I'm not running away from us anymore. I don't want to have to hide. I want my family to know. I want everyone to know. I'll deal with the consequences, all right?"

"We'll deal together," I corrected.

"We will. But most importantly, I'll have you."

I wove my fingers together behind his neck and tugged him down until our lips nearly touched. "You've always had me."

And then he kissed me, long and hard and full of promise.

6

____

HARLEY

Our grumbling stomachs drove us back into town. My wet hair was in a hasty ponytail on my head. I left my black jean shorts unbuttoned and rolled down to reveal the wet bottoms beneath. I went without my shirt, just my bikini top. Chase was seated on a towel. His blue shirt clinging to his tan skin. Bowie was in the back of the Subaru with his tongue lolling out the window.

We dropped the dog off at Chase's house before driving back to mine so I could get a change of clothes. He'd stayed the night at my place the night before, and I had every intention of staying the night at his. But I had my first day at Wright tomorrow and needed work attire.

Chase followed me out of the car, locking it behind us as I all but skipped up the sidewalk.

"We're going to have to figure out how to get Bowie to stay at my house," I told him.

"Does Bailey like dogs?"

"She'd better. We don't really have a backyard, so it might be cramped."

"And Bowie is a lot."

I shrugged. "He's the best. Just like his namesake."

He laughed as I fit the key into the lock and turned the door handle. I stepped inside with Chase on my heels and nearly skidded to a stop in the doorway.

My throat closed as I saw the man standing in my living room. "Owen?"

"Hey, honey," my dad said.

Chase froze behind me. I could practically feel his shock as he closed the door firmly behind him. He cleared his throat. He stepped forward and offered his hand. "Hello, sir."

"Sinclair," Owen said, shaking his hand.

I still hadn't moved.

"What are you doing here?"

Owen released Chase's hand, and that was when I saw his mask drop. Just a split second, but long enough for me to recognize it. It was the same emotions I kept locked up tight from years of learning from the best. But he couldn't hide from me any more than I could hide from him.

He was *furious*.

Beyond furious.

He was practically murderous with anger. How quickly had he left Vancouver to get here the next day after discovering I'd withdrawn? I'd blocked him, along with my brothers yesterday afternoon. It was a long-ass flight for him to make it that quickly.

He'd thought that he'd won. I was going to Harvard Law. Even better, he'd gotten Jordan to respond to him. We all knew that Jordan was his favorite. He might not have admitted it, but it was obvious to anyone involved. Now, Jordan wasn't talking to him. No one was talking to him. And I wasn't going to Harvard.

"I came to fix this situation," Owen said.

"How did you even get inside?"

"I have a key," he said as if it were obvious. "I own the building."

My jaw dropped. "What?"

"What? You thought I'd let you live anywhere? Of course not."

I shook my head. It was dizzy with anger at the realization. He would never stop. He would go and go and go until he got what he wanted. Whether that was Harvard or my living situation or anything. If he wanted it, he'd manipulate to get it.

"You're unbelievable."

"I will always take care of you."

"I don't *want* you to take care of me," I snapped. "That is the whole point."

He shook his head. "You're acting like a child. I know you're smarter than this."

"I'm smart enough to know that I made the right decision blocking your number and having my brothers do the same."

"Ah," he said slowly. "Is that why I can't reach them anymore?"

"Yes! Because you refuse to stop meddling."

"Meddling? You mean, taking care of my daughter," he argued.

"Taking care of me isn't *ratting* me out to my brothers when I don't fall into line."

Owen clenched his jaw. "We had a deal, you and I. You broke your end of the deal."

"Are you insane? If you're supposed to be my father, you don't make stupid, manipulative deals with your daughter to get what you want. You just parent. But fuck, you can't even do that."

"I will do whatever it takes," Owen said unrepentantly.

My eyes shot to Chase's as fury coursed through me. He tipped his head at me, letting me know without words that he was here for me. That nothing was going to change whatever Owen said, that I could get through this conversation. I took a breath of relief at the fortification in that look.

"You will never change."

He shrugged. "If you want me to be the villain, then fine, Harley. But we *are* going to talk about this Harvard situation."

"What situation?" I demanded. "Because as far as I'm concerned, it's settled."

"I called Harvard yesterday to make a payment and was informed that you *withdrew*."

"That's right," I said, holding my head up.

"You've worked your entire life for this. You took that LSAT course. You got top marks on the exam and maintained a 4.0, and for what?"

I straightened my spine and told him what I should have told him a long time ago. "I don't want to be a lawyer."

"Since when?" he demanded.

"For a long time," I finally admitted on a sigh. "For so

very long. But I just kept going because it felt like it was the right thing to do. It was what I'd said I wanted, right? I worked so hard. So, I had to do it."

"Yes, you do. You can't throw it all away."

"I'm not throwing anything away," I argued. "I'm just taking a different path."

"For him," Owen snarled.

Chase held his hands up. "I had no part in this. I encouraged her to go."

"He did."

"Sure. And you're now together, and somehow, you're staying in Lubbock."

"We weren't together when I made that decision. And while, yes, it's a perk that Chase is here"—I shot him a reassuring smile—"it changes nothing."

"It changes everything." He shook his head. "You're lucky that I know someone on the board of admissions."

"You what?" I asked in confusion.

Owen nodded. "I called my friend to see if there was anything that could be done. Since you're such an exceptional candidate, they agreed that they would remove your withdrawal from their records and you could start in the fall."

I blinked at him. Was he serious? He hadn't heard a word that I just said.

"I don't want that."

"It's the right thing to do." Then, he turned to Chase, giving him the stern look that said he was about to try a new level of manipulation. "Tell her. You went to law school. How many doors would Harvard Law open?"

"I'm not here to get between you and your daughter," he said, stepping to my side. "I'm only on her side."

"You're not an idiot, Sinclair. You went to Yale. You know what that did for you. Do you really want to hinder her here?"

"I understand that Harvard Law opens doors, but I'm not going to make her do anything she doesn't want to. Going to law school because you're supposed to and not because you want to be a lawyer is a recipe for disaster. I watched people burn out. There was a suicide case my 1L year, in fact. It's not uncommon. I'm not risking her in any way."

My stomach twisted at those words. I'd never heard him talk about law school like that. He'd esteemed its pros to me, and I'd thought long and hard about its cons, but I hadn't thought that it was so tough that people killed themselves. I couldn't imagine that being my reality, but it was still terrifying.

Owen clenched his jaw, as if irritated that his new line of questioning wasn't working out. "That would never happen to Harley."

"It wouldn't," I agreed. "Because I'm not going."

Owen huffed. "What are you going to do instead? You have nothing lined up other than this. You have never taken my money, so you have no savings. Are you living off of Sinclair now?" he sneered.

"I got a job," I said with a shrug. "At the company of my namesake."

He startled at that. "You're going to work at Wright Construction? Doing what?"

"I'm going to work in diversity and inclusion."

He waved his hand, making a *psh* sound. "That's bull-shit, Harley. You know it is. You're better than that. Get the law degree, start in upper management, and take over as CEO from Morgan in a few years."

My body shuddered with anger at those words. "First, you dismissed what I want. Then, you dismissed my job. And then, the cherry on top, *Dad*"—I said the word like a slur—"you make your intentions clear."

"Which are?"

"Your petty fucking revenge."

His nostrils flared. "None of this has anything to do with me."

I laughed. "Sure. You were the son who was sent away to work in Vancouver. Even after your brother died, you didn't get the CEO position. It went to Jensen, his son, who you thought was too young. Then, he stepped down. It all looked like a clear path to your ascension, and what happened? Morgan took over. And you couldn't stand for that, so you tried to sabotage her taking the reins. Which inevitably landed you in deep shit. Now, you're trying to use *me* to get the position you always wanted." I crossed my arms over my chest. "What, Jordan and Whitt wouldn't do your little mastermind takeover plan, so you found another path?"

"That is outlandish," he argued.

"Makes perfect sense to me," Chase said.

"Doesn't it?"

"I just want you to have the best life you could have."

"Even if I believed that," I said on a scoff, "which I do not, I'm telling you, that life is not for me. I'm in front of you right now, saying I want something else. And if it's a mistake, then it's *my* mistake to make."

"I don't have to accept that."

I smiled, a deadly thing that I'd mastered from him. I might hate him, but he'd given me the teeth to see this conversation to its inevitable conclusion.

"You don't get a say. Not anymore."

"Your mother clearly thinks that I do. She was the one who called and told me what happened with your brothers." He glanced at Chase's black eye. "She was not pleased with any of this." He tensed at his own words, and I saw what he wasn't saying.

I saw the final blow that explained his desperate flight out here.

"She's mad at you," I muttered.

He stiffened, clearly irritated that I could read him so well. "She wanted me to fix this."

I laughed. "Oh, I'm sure that's what she said. Tell the truth, Owen. Mom is also over your shit."

"My relationship with your mother is complicated."

"Oh, this is great," I said with a laugh. "You're so desperate that it reeks."

He ground his teeth together. "I am trying to *fix* this, Harley."

But he wasn't. He was just trying to save his own skin. Same old, same old.

"The boys cut you out. I cut you out. And now, Mom has, too." I nodded my head at him and then went to the door. "This is what you deserve, you know? You did this to yourself."

"Harley..."

"This is good-bye." I opened the door. "Oh, and I'm moving out of this house. Keep your grubby hands out of my life, Owen."

He looked like he was going to argue, but Chase put his hand on his shoulder and gently moved him toward the door. "You heard the lady."

Owen looked back at me after stepping across the threshold. "I do want what's best for everyone."

"You want what's best for you," I corrected him. "And we're done with your shit."

Then, I closed the door in his face.

Chase's arms were around me a second later, and I buried my face into his shoulder. He brushed his hands down my back. Then pulled me back, cupping my jaw in his hands.

"I'm proud of you. How are you feeling?"

"Powerful," I admitted. "I think it's finally over."

"I think so, too."

"He's just despicable. The house situation—"

I glanced around the house I'd called a home for two years, and he'd just yanked it out from under me. Bailey and I had only casually discussed what we were going to do for next year. She'd be starting her junior year, and I'd be working full-time. Now, it seemed impossible.

"I don't know where I'm going to live."

He blew out a breath. "Well, you could stay with me until you figure it out."

My eyes jumped to him in surprise. "Are you serious?"

"Of course. I'm not letting you stay here or move in

with your brothers unless that's something you want to do."

"No," I said quickly.

"I didn't think so." He pressed a kiss to my forehead. "We'll figure it out. For now, you can stay with me."

"Okay," I whispered, finding the whole thing almost unbelievable. I circled his waist and drew in his sunscreen scent. "I'm glad you were here for all of this."

"Always, baby girl. Always."

PART II

NOW THAT YOU KNOW

7

CHASE

My mom fluffed her freshly dyed blonde hair on the video chat. "What do you think, dear?"

"It looks good, Mom. Are we still on for lunch next week?"

"Sure. Sure. I have to rearrange some things. Busy schedule and all."

Ever since the divorce, my mom's schedule had gotten shockingly busy. So much that I rarely saw her unless she penned me in. I had a feeling this was her way of dating without telling me about it. Which I honestly appreciated. And she had every right to go out and find someone better than my dad. But it was also just weird.

"Sure. I just really wanted to talk to you about something."

I'd been trying all week to reach her. I wanted her to meet Harley. I figured starting with my mom was the best way to go since she was the least likely to care about the Wrights now that the divorce was final.

"What is this all about, dear? Can't you just tell me

now? We can still get lunch, but you look anxious. Not good for your complexion. You're going to get lines in your forehead." She pinched her unmoving forehead. "Of course, that looks good on a man." It was said bitterly.

"I'm not anxious. I just have exciting news. Someone that I want you to meet."

Her eyes widened. "Someone to meet. Who?"

"Can I introduce you at lunch?"

My mom pursed her lips. "I don't like surprises, Chase. You know I've had enough for a lifetime."

Yeah, she had.

All the girls my dad had cheated on her with. Not to mention the new baby that he'd had with his mistress. While I found Silas to be the cutest one-year-old around —he was my half-brother after all—every other aspect of his existence disgusted me. The fact that Dayna had been an employee at Sinclair Realty when she was knocked up. That the board hadn't fired my father, but just made me the face of the company while he worked in the background. How my father hadn't legitimized his relationship with Dayna by marrying the poor girl, who was *younger* than me.

Maybe I owed my mother not to surprise her with the fact that I was dating a Wright. I didn't think she would be as upset as, say, my father, but I never really knew.

"I've started seeing someone," I admitted slowly.

Her smile lit up. "Have you? Is it serious?"

"It is," I told her, unable to keep the joy out of my voice. "She's sort of moved in."

"Already, Chase? That's moving fast for you. You

dated Kennedy for three *years* before she moved in with you."

Ah, Kennedy. That name I hadn't thought about in a long time. My Houston girlfriend, who had wanted nothing more than to live in my house and be my wife and tell all of her friends that we had hit new milestones. That felt like a lifetime ago.

"It's not fast exactly, but it does feel right."

"If you say so, dear. Moving in before I've even met the girl doesn't sound like you."

"This is a special circumstance. We've sort of been seeing each other for three years, but we've just made it official."

Her eyes widened. "Excuse me? Did you say three *years*?"

"I only say that to show you that this isn't a spur-of-the-moment decision. I love her, and I want you to meet her."

"And who is this girl?"

I took a deep breath. Here goes nothing.

"Harley Wright."

A shriek sounded from behind my mother, who went pale and wide-eyed.

I blinked. "Is there someone there with you?"

My mom turned her iPad from where she stood in her living room to my sister, who had been carefully off-screen in the kitchen. My stomach turned to ice.

"Ashleigh," I muttered.

Fuck.

I hadn't wanted to tell my sister yet.

She was...a gossip at best. A meddling, opinionated

saboteur at worst. And she sided with our dad as much as she sided with Mom. I didn't trust her not to tell him, and I wanted to do that on my own time.

"You're dating Harley Wright?" Ashleigh asked, scurrying toward the camera and practically yanking it out of Mom's hands.

"I am," I said very slowly, guarded.

"For three *years*?" she gasped.

"On and off."

"Oh. My. God, this is too much. How did you keep this from me for so long?"

"On purpose," I mumbled under my breath.

"Chase! She's a *Wright*."

"I'm aware."

"I dated a Wright."

"I am also aware of that," I told her.

And she had royally fucked that up. She'd been with Julian for two years before he found out the depths of her subterfuge. I didn't know how he'd made it that long.

"Well, that's great," Mom interjected. She wiggled her fingers at Ashleigh to get back in the camera. "Does your father know?"

"He...does not. Not yet," I said carefully. "I want to be the one to tell him."

"Of course, dear. We wouldn't dream of ruining that moment for you."

Ashleigh bit her lip like she could barely contain shouting it to the entire world.

"Right, Ashleigh?" Mom said.

She huffed. "Fine. *Fine.* I won't mention it to Dad."

"Or anyone who will tell your father," Mom added.

"Chase deserves a chance to have his father yell at him all alone the first time."

I could barely suppress the laughter that bubbled up at me at those words. "Thanks, I think."

"Dad's going to flip," Ashleigh said. "You know he is. It's a *Wright*. After what happened at Jensen's mayoral campaign..."

I shrugged. "That sounds like a him problem."

"Your sister is right, of course. He will not be thrilled, but if you're happy, that is all that matters. Do you know when you're going to tell him? And can I be there to see his face?"

"Mom!" Ashleigh gushed.

This time, I did laugh. Oh, my mom hated him so much.

"It was a joke, darling," Mom said with laughter in her eyes. "Don't take everything so seriously."

"The humor looks good on you."

Mom fluffed her hair again. "Everything looks good on me." She winked at me through the camera. "Now, how is *her* family taking it?"

I blew out a heavy breath. "Well, they hate me. Her brothers especially."

My black eye had healed, for which I was glad. I wasn't sure I wanted my mom to know that Jordan had punched me. But Ashleigh was staring intently through the camera, as if she could see through the healed skin to what had happened.

"Well, it's hard to blame them. We've given them plenty of reasons to hate us. As they have given us plenty of reasons to hate them."

"I guess," I said doubtfully. "Anyway, I am on my way to her soccer game now. So, I'm going to go deal with their hatred."

"Chin up, dear. You're a Sinclair."

"Thanks, Mom."

"And let's do lunch, like you suggested. Next week sometime works in my schedule."

"Sounds good," I agreed.

"I'm having a girls' weekend soon," Ashleigh blurted out before I could go. "Like, in two weeks. We're doing a spa day and going out for drinks."

My eyebrows rose. "Okay?"

"Harley should come. I want to get to know her."

I hesitated over that. "I'll have to ask her if she's interested."

"Do that, brother of mine. And then give me her number so I can make plans when she says yes."

"Right," I said uncertainly.

Ashleigh was being nice. Maybe too nice. I wasn't sure what to think of it. Was it sincere, or was it Ashleigh being Ashleigh? I'd have to run it by Harley and see what she thought.

"I'll talk to y'all later," I said, making my excuse to get off the phone.

I pulled a baseball cap on my head and headed out the door. The outdoor soccer complex was only ten minutes from my house. I parked the Subaru near the back, walking the long way to the fields. My mom had been right. I was anxious. Not about Harley. She and I were perfect. Having her at the house was like waking up in a dream every day. I'd wanted this—her—for so long that it was like she fit right in where I'd always assumed she would.

But I was nervous about her brothers.

Enduring their hatred.

Hoping to win them over.

Knowing that it was unlikely.

I released a harsh breath. It didn't matter. I was going to this game regardless. I was here for my girlfriend. And I would keep coming back and dealing with their ire, no matter what happened. They were going to learn that they couldn't run me off.

Harley was on the field, dribbling a soccer ball when I arrived. I picked her out from a dozen yards with her ice-blonde hair up in a high ponytail. She kicked the ball to Annie, who did some impressive footwork and then lobbed it back.

Bailey waved from the stands when she saw me. "Sinclair, over here!"

Ah, Bailey, so subtle.

A sea of heads turned in my direction.

Jordan and Whitt were seated together. Julian was on the field. While West had gone back on tour with Cosmere, leading up to his and Nora's wedding next month. But there were other Wrights in attendance. Sutton Wright was seated with Julian's wife, Jennifer. Jensen was there as well since his oldest son, Colton, played on the team. He was an eighteen-year-old superstar who had taken to all the sports in his school like waves to water. Harley bragged on him a lot. That he'd been recruited in both football and track even though, apparently, he really wanted to play soccer. He gotten into as many top universities as she had and would be attending Harvard in the fall. She'd admitted that she was sad they wouldn't be there at the same time. Though it was the only thing she was sad about.

I waved at Bailey and climbed into the stands to sit next to her and Eve. "Hey, Bailey."

"Hey, Chase!" she said, just as loud and dramatic as the first time.

Eve snorted next to her. "Bails, cut it out. The guy looks like he's going to hyperventilate."

"I'm fine," I told her. "Good to see you, Eve."

"Surprised you're here," Whitt said from her other side.

I met his gaze. "Why wouldn't I be?"

He shrugged and leaned back. Right.

Eve smacked him. "Whitt, I swear."

He pressed a kiss to her cheek and said in just above a whisper, "I promised I'd try to be nice."

Jordan's gaze landed on me. "I didn't."

I tipped my head at him in acknowledgment. Glad that there were three people between us. I didn't have to be here, but I was here for Harley. As long as he didn't punch me again, this would be fine.

Harley found me in the stands as she ran over to the sidelines for the game to begin. She waved high and wide in my direction. I laughed and waved back. She blew me a kiss before following the team out onto the pitch.

I relaxed as the game went on. Bailey kept up a steady stream of commentary on the match. It was appreciated, as it kept me from having to say much of anything to anyone else there. We were all playing nice, but we weren't suddenly happy about the situation.

Julian moved into position to take a corner kick. I found Harley standing right smack in the middle of the group, ready for what was coming their way. They were down, two to one, despite Colton and Blaire doing their most to try to score. The teams were evenly matched.

We all held our breath as Julian prepped the ball. This was the end of the first half, and a goal here—especially a goal from one of the girls, which counted for two —would put them in a much better position, going into halftime.

Julian's kick soared through the air. Even I could admit that it was perfect, directly where he'd wanted it to land—in the center of the cluster of players. It came toward Harley. I watched her decision to go for it. Everyone jumped at once. She and a guy nearly a head taller than her arced up into the air.

The guy reared back, slamming his head into Harley's as he went for the soccer ball. It grazed off of his head and out of the way of the goal. The crowd booed, the players looked frustrated, and Harley fell.

I was on my feet as soon as I watched her body go limp. The guy who'd headbutted her was already jogging away, oblivious to her landing at his feet. A gasp went up from the stands. Julian ran forward, and the rest of the team was already heading that way.

I didn't know what compelled me, but I couldn't just stand there and watch it happen. I was running across the pitch before the ref even blew the whistle for the end of the half.

8

———————

HARLEY

The light was blinding when I opened my eyes. I winced and quickly shut them again. I groaned as little stars flickered around my eyelids.

Fuck, what had happened?

"Hey, hey, I'm here," Chase said.

His hand was holding mine. I could feel him hovering over me. There was worry in his voice.

"What...happened?" I croaked.

"You got hit in the head at the game. Do you remember that?"

My eyes opened to slits. "The game. Right."

I was still lying on the grass on the field. I didn't know how long I'd been out, but it all came back to me quickly. The corner kick that had resulted in that huge lug of a guy headbutting me when we both went for the header.

"I don't feel too good."

"It's all right," he said reassuringly.

"No, I—" But the words never left my mouth. I turned

over and vomited up my guts. I choked on how gross that was as I heaved onto the grass in front of the goal. My stomach tightened as I expelled my hastily eaten dinner.

"Concussion," a voice said over me.

"Fuck," Chase said. "You think so?"

"Oh, definitely."

I winced and rolled back over to see Annie kneeling on the other side while the rest of the team looked on.

"You think I have a concussion?"

"Well, I'd have looked at you, but Chase barreled me out of the way. Guess we don't need the doctor in the house," she joked. Her smile alight for him. She looked genuinely happy that he was out on the pitch.

Chase shot her an exasperated look. "Is she going to be okay?"

"Yeah. Sure. She seems pretty with it. I'd recommend ice and resting the next day or two." She nodded at Chase. "I expect you to enforce my rules. No wild activity this weekend."

He scowled at her. "Ruin my fun."

She bit her lip to keep from laughing. "I'll mention that to Jordan later."

"Please don't," I said weakly. "And can someone help me up?"

Chase got his arm underneath me and gradually helped me to my feet. I wiped my mouth with the back of my hand. I was a little dizzy, but it wasn't enough that I couldn't walk or anything.

The guy who'd run into me ran over and apologized, but I waved him off. I didn't think he had done it intentionally. Just bad luck. But it definitely meant I was out the rest of the game.

Chase kept his arm around me as we walked off the field and right into the bulk of my family.

"Are you okay?" Bailey asked. "That looked terrible. You dropped like a sack of potatoes."

"Thanks, Bails. I'm fine."

"She has a concussion," Chase said. "I'm going to take her home and get her some ice and rest."

"My knight in shining armor," I said with only half a laugh. Because when I laughed, my head hurt, and I winced.

"Jesus, Harley, do you need to go to the hospital?" Whitt asked. He looked like he'd had a shock to his system when I fell.

"No hospital. Not when there's an ER doctor on the field."

"What did Annie say?" Jordan asked.

"Just that I seemed with it and I should rest. It's no big deal, y'all."

"You threw up on the field," Whitt said.

"You should have seen the way you collapsed," Jordan said.

"It was really scary," Eve agreed.

"I'm fine. Chase is going to take care of me."

Jordan looked like he'd just eaten a lemon, but he stuck his hand out to Chase. He eyed it warily before putting his hand in Jordan's to shake. "I saw the look on your face when you realized she was hurt. Take care of her."

"I intend to."

Whitt huffed. "You can sprint—that's for sure."

Eve elbowed him. "Be nice."

"Let us know how she's doing, okay?" he added on hastily.

Chase nodded at them both. "I'll take care of her."

"I am *right* here," I reminded them. "Perfectly capable of taking care of myself. You do not need to infantilize me just because you realized Chase isn't the douchebag you had decided he was in your head."

"Nice, Harley," Whitt said with a laugh.

Jordan shrugged and held his hands up. "Just playing nice."

"Y'all are rich," Bailey said. "Get some sleep, sis. Text if you need anything."

"Will do."

Then, I was leaning on Chase's arm, and he walked me out to his car. I'd driven in with Bailey. So, it was lucky that I didn't have to abandon my little Kia.

Once I was in the passenger seat, I said, "I think you just won my brothers over."

He shot me a disbelieving look. "I don't think I'd go that far."

"Nah, Jordan shook your hand."

"It doesn't matter. All I care about is how you are feeling." His hand came to my face. "It was fucking terrifying watching you drop like that."

I touched his hand. "I'm fine. I'm sure it was nothing."

"It was not nothing. It was horrible, and I never want to see you hurt again."

He leaned in like he was going to kiss me.

I balked and reared back. "I just threw up."

"And?"

"And I am disgusting."

He shot me a bemused look. "Harley, you are never disgusting to me."

"My breath is gross. You don't want to—"

But then his lips were on mine, and he kissed me so long and hard that I thought maybe I was going to black out again.

"I do want to," he said when he pulled back. "I always want to."

My heart fluttered at his words. He'd just careened across a soccer pitch, thrown his best friend out of the way, and stood up for me in front of my brothers. Now, he was taking care of me and being so fucking sweet. And I thought I was going to die of happiness. Even with the concussion.

"Careful," he teased. "I know that look."

"What look?" I asked, my voice going breathy.

"That is the look you give me right before you do something devious."

"I don't know what you're talking about."

"Usually, you proceed to fuck my brains out."

"Well, who can blame me?"

He laughed. "Like I said, careful. You have to rest. You heard Annie—no wild activity."

"Fine. We can be all saint-like and missionary about it. Nothing wild at all."

He sputtered on another laugh. "The way that mind works."

He revved the engine and pulled away from the fields.

"You say that like it's a bad thing."

"Oh no, it's a fucking wonderful thing. Hottest thing about you."

"Better than me in my Harley Quinn outfit?" I teased.

He choked. "I refuse to speculate. You might have to show it to me again so I can decide."

I giggled, but that made my head hurt. So, I decided Annie was probably right and I should have a chill weekend. Even if the thought of cosplaying Harley Quinn and getting fucked in pigtails was pretty enticing. Unfortunately, it was not exactly reasonable in my current condition.

We made it back to Chase's house, and he helped me inside, putting me on the couch and getting ice for my head.

"You look cute in a baseball cap," I said when Chase handed me two Tylenol and a water to help with my headache. "I don't think I've ever seen you in one."

He pulled it off and flipped it around, putting it backward on his head. "Yeah, I used to wear them a lot and then gave up the habit."

"Mmm." I gestured for him to come closer. "It's even hotter backward."

He chuckled. "You are trying to get me in trouble."

"Do you have gray sweatpants too?"

"I don't even want to know, do I?"

My eyes drifted to the crotch of his pants and back up to his eyes. Then, I winked.

He shook his head. "You're objectifying me. I am a strong, independent man, Harley Wright. I am more than just my body."

I couldn't keep from laughing that time. He'd heard me say something similar one too many times if he was quoting it back at me.

"My bad. I will think of something other than having your cock inside of me."

He dropped onto the couch next to me and slanted our lips together. "Please don't."

I moaned against him as I reached for his pants, and a wave of dizziness overtook me. He pushed me gently backward on the sofa.

"Rest. We have time for that later."

"Not fair."

"You're going to make yourself throw up," he reminded me. "Again."

I sighed and settled back into the couch. "So, did you ever hear from your mom about lunch or whatever?"

He scratched his neck and looked guilty. "Um...about that."

"What happened?"

"Well, I decided to tell her about you because I figured she'd had enough surprises from my dad."

"Okay," I drawled.

"And she was okay with it."

"Good," I said, waiting for the other shoe to drop.

"But Ashleigh was at her house and overheard."

I winced and reeled back from that. We'd planned to tell Ashleigh, of course, but she was complicated. Chase had given me a full pros and cons list about when to tell Ashleigh. Personally, I didn't care, but he did, and I just wanted to do whatever would be the easiest. I hadn't expected this.

"And she's not okay with it?"

"I don't know," he admitted. "I mean, she freaked out. Screamed at the top of her lungs. But Mom convinced her not to tell my dad since I said that I wanted to."

"Which is good."

"She seemed very...nice about it."

"Nice is also good."

"I don't know," he said again.

I laughed and touched my aching head. "Just spit it out. What's bothering you? You afraid your sister won't like me? I mean, isn't that par for the course?"

"She invited you to a girls' weekend actually."

"A girls' weekend?" I asked in surprise.

"Yeah, a spa day and drinks. It's a whole thing. She does them regularly with her friends."

I had been prepared for Ashleigh to dislike me. I hadn't been prepared for her to invite me to parties and shit. Did she want to get to know me? Or did she want to sniff out information? I'd heard enough about her from Julian to know she was treacherous. I just didn't know where this fell into place.

"Should I go?"

"Do you want to go?" he asked.

"I mean, I could use a spa day if that's what you're asking, but is she being sincere?"

"I really wish I knew the answer to that. I never quite know where Ashleigh falls. And you don't have to go if you're worried about it."

"I'm not worried. I can handle myself," I insisted. "I just want to make sure I'm coming into this on the right footing."

"I don't want you to handle yourself. You know what?" he said with a headshake, coming to his feet. "I'll just tell her no."

"Wait, I didn't say no."

"She's probably going to try to do something stupid. Her friends are all catty. I don't know if you'd like any of them."

"Hold up." I held my hand out. "I can handle a spa day with other girls. I want to get to know your sister, too. I'm sure she's not as bad as everyone makes her out to be. Maybe she just needs a real friend."

"That is very sweet," he said with a frown. "But I'm not sure it's reality with Ashleigh."

I laughed. "How bad can it be?"

"That I do not want the answer to."

"Well, I don't have to go if you don't want me to get to know your sister. But I don't think she's going to just leave us alone if I say no," I reasoned.

I watched him contemplate that answer. I had memorized all the lines of his face. And even just being in his house for the last week had been enough for me to begin to learn that every movement he made had a story to tell. He was debating now whether or not it was worth it to deal with Ashleigh now or later.

"Fine. Fine," he said, giving in. "I'll tell her you'll go. But if you need to bail, I can come get you at any time."

"I'll be fine," I said on a laugh. "Honestly, you act like she's going to cut me in my sleep."

"No, she's never that direct," he muttered.

"Chase, get down here and kiss me and stop worrying about your sister. It'll be fine."

He dropped back onto the couch and brought our lips together again, but I could feel wariness in him. I hoped that he was wrong and Ashleigh was just dramatic. I'd dealt with girls like her back home and in college. Nothing I couldn't handle.

9

———

HARLEY

"Drinks tonight?" Courtney called over to me as I stepped out of my office for the day.

I laughed and shook my head. "Can't tonight. I have a thing with Chase's sister."

Courtney wheeled over to where I was standing. "Ohhh," she said, "family time."

"Not exactly. We're going to some spa in the middle of nowhere. That's actually why I'm cutting out a little early. I have to drive out there."

"Oh my God, are you talking about The Retreat?"

"Yes," I said.

She directed her wheelchair down the hallway toward the elevator with me. "I heard it's fucking magical. Also a fortune but amazing."

"Well, I guess it's good to know that it's real."

It was hard to admit that I'd been worried his sister was going to send me on a wild goose chase. Chase had spooked me enough about his sister to think that she'd do it. Julian had only made it worse when I asked him about his ex-girlfriend. But apparently, I'd just let them get in my head.

Thankfully, Courtney was bringing me back down to reality.

We'd clicked the first day that I stepped foot into Wright Construction. She was a bubbly ball of light and only a few years older than me. Destined for upper management as far as I was concerned.

"Well, next time," Courtney said. "I'm so glad you decided to take this job, Harley. You're such an asset to the team. I hope you know that."

I flushed with approval at those words. "Thanks, girl. The feeling is absolutely mutual."

I waved good-bye once we got out to the parking lot, a little skip in my step. See, I'd made the right choice. I was doing the right thing. At least that part of my life seemed to be on track despite the clusterfuck it had caused personally. Plus, I got to be with Chase.

If only I didn't have this spa day planned. Why had I agreed to this again?

I got behind the wheel of my Kia, turned David Bowie on full blast, and headed out into the middle of nowhere.

The spa appeared on the horizon like an apparition. It was surrounded on all sides by a sea of scrubby grass and quintessential Lubbock tumbleweeds. Just a large mosaic-dotted building in a long, flat line of nothing. I parked out front, amid the BMWs, Mercedes, and Range Rovers.

I could barely stop my jaw from unhinging at the sight of the interior. The lobby was three stories high with tinkling water coming down a waterfall against one wall. The place was otherwise minimalist and pure white on every surface with a view of the arid climate beyond.

"Welcome to The Retreat on the Permian Basin. Can I help you?"

"Yes, I'm here for a group spa day. It's reserved under Ashleigh Sinclair."

"Oh, yes. Ashleigh is one of our most dedicated clients. And your name is?"

"Harley. Harley Wright."

"Excellent. You're on the guest list."

The woman got my shoe and robe size and then directed me through the maze of a building to a changing area. I stripped down to nothing but the robe and comfortable rubber shoes. It took me longer than I'd thought because I was struck by the row upon row of glass paned showers, a blow-dry bar, a shaving bar, a full circle of mirrors with everything from hair products to makeup to perfumes and beyond.

The woman was waiting for me when I finally came back out. She showed me the rows of saunas and jetted hot tubs before directing me to a personal quiet room for Ashleigh's party.

I took a deep breath and then went inside. Ashleigh was on a circular lounge chair in the dimly lit room, seated at the center of all of her adoring friends, as if she were a queen on her throne. Every unfamiliar person in that room had to be eight to ten years older than me. And when I was with Chase, I never felt like that mattered, but in that moment, I felt...young.

I didn't like it.

I was saved from having to make some grand entrance by someone I *did* recognize.

"Harley!"

"Elsie," I said in surprise.

Kai's wife and I had met at the Cosmere show a few years ago, and Chase and I had gone out to dinner with them last week. She was wonderfully down-to-earth and made my heart stop racing almost immediately. I would be fine. Why had I even been worried?

"I'm so glad you made it!"

"Me too."

"Oh, Harley!" Ashleigh said with a little giggle at the end. "Welcome to The Retreat. This is my home away from home."

"It's nice," I said truthfully.

It was nicer than anywhere I'd ever been before. In fact, it was pretty out of my tax bracket. I might be a Wright with a trust fund, but I didn't fucking touch the thing. Money from Owen was off-limits. Not unless I was desperate—and a spa day did not count.

"Everyone, this is Harley Wright." She gestured to me. "Harley, these are all my best friends."

She listed off a dozen names in quick succession, and I wasn't sure I was going to remember anyone but Elsie. But I smile and waved.

"Nice to meet all of you," I said.

"Harley is dating Chase, and so we have to be extra nice to her. My big brother's new girlfriend deserves only the best." She raised a mimosa in my honor.

My cheeks heated at the words. I couldn't quite tell if she was being nice or making fun of me. Julian had said she had that way about her, but still, it was disarming to witness it firsthand.

"Thanks," I said with a smile.

"Do you want a drink?" one of the minions asked.

The second girl touched the first's arm. "Wait, are you old enough to drink?"

Someone snickered behind a hand.

Oh, lovely.

"Yep. Old enough to drink," I said with a forced smile.

"We weren't sure. You look like such a baby," the first said.

"Good genes," I quipped.

"I mean, obviously," Ashleigh said. "Those Wrights and their eternal youth."

Again, was that a compliment? Or did she hate us as much as my family hated hers?

"We're lucky like that," I said, trying for nonchalance.

"Luck," another girl said with a laugh. "Or the money from a Fortune 500."

A girl flattened a finger down her nose. "Whoever did yours was incredible."

"Agreed. Oh my God, I was just going to say the same," another girl said. "You'll have to give us your surgeon's name. Are they here in Lubbock or back where you're from? Where is that again?"

"Seattle," Ashleigh filled in.

"Surgeon?" I asked in confusion.

"Y'all," Elsie said with an eye roll. She met my uncertain look. "They want to fix their botched nose jobs."

A gasp came from the girls.

"I didn't say ours were botched!"

"I'll give you the name," I said even though I'd never had a nose job myself. "If you need the help."

Ashleigh laughed as if the chaos was where she thrived. "Oh, I like you. I see why brother dearest likes you, too."

Elsie huffed next to me. "Ashleigh."

"She's fine, Els. Don't hover like my mother." Ashleigh winked at me. "We're just having fun, aren't we?"

"Sure," I said because what else could I say?

Elsie looked uncertainly between us. "Come on. You can sit with me."

I took a seat next to her on a chaise and accepted a mimosa. My hands were a little shaky as I took a sip of the champagne. I could stand up to much more formidable foes, but I felt that same little girl shit I'd felt growing up when the cool girls looked down on me. Turned out, people in high school didn't like when you were confident. Correction: people anywhere.

I was only seated a minute before the door opened and names were called. I jumped from my seat and followed the masseuse for my first of many treatments. Ashleigh had scheduled a massage and facial for every girl. Plus professional hair and makeup before we went out. There were optional add-ons that I was sure many of the girls were getting, but I wasn't sure I needed a body scrub or a manicure or red-light therapy. Or at least my wallet said I didn't.

I had to hand it to Ashleigh though. There was a reason this place cost a fortune. It was easily the best massage I had ever had in my life. I left the table feeling dizzy with the release of tension. My hips in particular holding all the tension from the new ice skates I'd purchased to use on the Tech ice. Not to mention my ankles. Ankles were not meant for new skates.

My facial was rejuvenating and mildly painful as the girl chemically peeled my face off. By the end, I looked like a glazed doughnut. Somehow in the best way. Yes, I was only twenty-two, but my skin *glowed* like it never had before. Apparently, it was the perfect base for the makeup artist, who declined my request for dark and smoky and heavy eyeliner for the softest, most natural look that I'd ever worn with the only concession being the winged liner. Combine that with the perfect blowout, and I somehow looked older. Also like I fit in with these other girls. It was disconcerting, to say the least.

When I finally made it back to the private room, there was only one other girl there. I didn't recognize her from when I'd first gotten here.

"Hey, is this still for Ashleigh?"

"Oh, yes, come in. I've been alone for ages. My fault for getting here early," she said with a laugh. "I absolutely need girl time. Sit. Sit." She patted her oversize chaise.

I crossed the room, wariness in my shoulders that the masseuse had just worked out. Was this girl like all the others? I'd handled myself just fine, but I didn't know if I needed to have my guard up.

"How was your service?" she asked, passing me a mimosa.

"The best ever," I admitted.

"I know, right? This is the best spa I've ever been to. Your first time?" she guessed.

"Yeah. Is it that obvious?"

"Nah, I just didn't recognize you. I've been coming to Ashleigh's retreats for a while. Most of the girls are pretty recycled, if you catch my drift." She laughed and brushed her shoulder-length blonde hair off of her shoulders. She had sideswept bangs and dark blue eyes, like she'd stepped out of a New England storm.

"I also got that impression."

"Ashleigh is sweet somewhere down deep," she told me. "She just hides it behind pettiness. And new girls always get the brunt of it. Don't take it personally."

"Thanks."

"You live in Lubbock?" she asked.

I nodded. "You?"

"Can you believe I fly in from Houston for these when I can? Just for this stupid spa."

"Houston?" I asked in surprise. "Wow. That is quite a trip for a spa."

"I've been seeing Klarissa for *years*. She's worth it to work out my soccer muscles."

"You play soccer?"

She nodded. "Not professional, mind you. I played in college and keep it up recreationally."

"Me too. Well, I didn't play in college, but I play recreationally with my family."

"I love that. It makes me so happy."

"I kind of suck," I said on a laugh. "I recently got a concussion."

"Fuck," she said. "I've had one too many of those.

And as I get older, it sure creeps up on you, you know?" Her eyes drifted down me. "How old *are* you?" She clapped her hand over her mouth. "That's so rude. You just look like twenty-five or something."

"Twenty-two actually," I said.

"Fuck," she said, tipping a mimosa to me. "I just turned thirty. I remember my twenty-two-year-old body. Do *not* take it for granted."

"Noted."

"Seriously shocked that Ashleigh would invite a twenty-two-year-old here. She usually refuses anyone prettier than her," she said with a laugh.

"But you're here," I said as if it were obvious.

She flushed. "Thank you, but I'm old guard, remember? You're fresh meat."

"Yeah, well, I'm still not sure if it was out of the goodness of her heart."

The girl rolled her eyes. "Nothing is out of the goodness of her heart."

That was fucking true.

Then, the door opened, and the queen bee herself sauntered inside. Her hair was bouncy and full of volume. Her makeup pristine. She looked like a goddess with her minions following in her wake.

"Oh, good! Harley, you met Kennedy!" Ashleigh said. "Kennedy, this is Chase's girlfriend, Harley."

Kennedy stiffened at those words. She set her champagne flute down a little harder than necessary. It was several stiff seconds before she glanced back at me with a hard smile.

"Sorry, you're dating Chase?" Kennedy asked in a

small voice.

"Um, yes," I said, glancing uneasily between Ashleigh and Kennedy. I wished that Elsie were here now to navigate this.

"Oh God, did I not mention that he and Kennedy dated for three years in Houston?"

My mouth opened slightly as understanding dawned. Kennedy. That Kennedy. He'd mentioned her name once in passing. She was Chase's ex. Well, shit.

"I see," I said softly.

"They were nearly *engaged*," Ashleigh went on.

"That's enough, Ashleigh," Kennedy barked. "She gets the picture."

Ashleigh had set this up. Was it to humiliate me or Kennedy? In that moment, I refused to let her win. She was hungry, waiting for the other shoe to drop. But I wouldn't give it to her. I could be confused and frustrated later.

I put my hand on hers. "Then, we must have so much in common."

Kennedy's eyes widened in surprise. When I enlarged my eyes and discreetly gestured to Ashleigh, she seemed to get the message.

"You're probably right." She laughed softly. "Thanks for bringing us together like this."

I held my drink up to Ashleigh like she'd done to me earlier. "Cheers."

Ashleigh was too poised to do anything but clap as if she were excited, but I watched her size me up. I didn't know what her deal was. Unfortunately, I had a feeling I was going to find out.

10

CHASE

"So, she's living with you," Kai said over a beer downtown.

"She is," I confirmed.

"And you're cool with that?"

"I hope she never leaves."

It was the truth. She'd been here for weeks, and I never wanted her out of my space. Something I still couldn't believe was my reality.

"Do you remember when Kennedy tried to just move in with you?" Kai asked. He barely suppressed a chuckle at my expense. "You were fucking furious. You wanted your space. You wanted bachelor pad status. You ranted for hours about this."

"Yeah, yeah," I grumbled.

Sometimes, it sucked having a friend who had seen me through all of my worsts. Between him and Annie, it was just a regular occasion of making fun of me.

"So, Harley is different?" Kai asked. "I mean, you two

seem great together when we went out the other day. And Elsie really likes her."

"I'm glad. Elsie is an excellent judge of character."

"Better than both of us."

I laughed. "So true."

"And she's living with you," he repeated as if he still couldn't believe it.

"She's the one."

"You bought Kennedy a ring," he reminded me.

I huffed in frustration. That was Kennedy's name two times in a matter of minutes, and I preferred when I forgot that she existed at all. "And I never gave it to her. I did it because it felt like I had to. We'd been together three years. She'd been living with me six months, and it was...fine. I didn't want to marry her though."

"Yeah, I know. It was good to see you wake up even if it was Annie who did the waking and then flattened your poor heart for Jordan Wright."

I held my beer up in the air. "Well, thanks to Annie, I am not married and have now met the one."

"About fucking time," Kai said.

"You can say that again."

I drained my beer, then lifted my hand for the bartender to bring us another round.

Kai's face drained of color.

"What?" I asked.

He slid his phone across the table. "Uh, I just got an SOS from Elsie. I think this is meant for you."

I furrowed my brow and then read the text message.

SOS, babe! Tell Chase that Kennedy is at Ashleigh's retreat this time.

I blinked at those words. My stomach dipped. Fucking Ashleigh.

I had known this was too good to be true. I'd known it, and I'd sent my girlfriend to the lion's den anyway. I swore she pissed me off. I was going to destroy her for this.

"We'll have the check instead," I said to the bartender.

"Ashleigh strikes again," Kai muttered.

"I'm going to kill her."

"That's what she wants, dude. You know she's hoping for a reaction from you."

"Then, she's going to fucking get it."

"Any excuse to tell your dad," Kai reminded me.

I closed my eyes as the fury roiled through me. Was that what this was? Was Ashleigh trying to find a reason to tell our dad? I wouldn't put it past her. But fuck, I *never* understood her motives. We'd grown up together in the same fucking house, and she was still a goddamn mystery. A selfish, unrepentant mystery.

"Should you call Harley?"

"I'll text her on the way."

"On the way?" Kai asked. He sighed. "Oh. We're going to interrupt girls' night."

"I'm not leaving Harley to deal with Ashleigh alone."

Kai tipped his beer back. "All right, let's go."

The bar that Ashleigh always took the girls after their spa day was attached to an upscale restaurant mere blocks from where Kai and I had been drinking. The girls usually had drinks and finger food and then went for a fancy dinner before ending up at the bar again afterward. She'd been doing these soirees for years.

Personally, I was surprised that Harley had even gone out with them after meeting Kennedy. She would have had to drive downtown from The Retreat. That was a solid thirty minutes to decide to remain. Also, she hadn't texted me. We'd only gotten the information from Elsie.

Where exactly was her head at?

Was she trying to one-up my sister? Was she staying to prove a point? I wouldn't put it past her, but I hoped that she didn't think I would want that. The last thing I wanted was for Ashleigh to make her uncomfortable.

So, I was unprepared for what I saw when I stepped inside.

My world narrowed to Harley. She was stunning on a normal day in sweats, her hair in a ponytail, just a swish of mascara. She was drop-dead gorgeous after the magic that spa had done to her. But she also looked...different.

She looked like she belonged in my sister's inner circle. More grown-up. Like I was seeing a glimpse of the woman that she would become. And I liked every inch of it. I was lucky that I would be the man to see it happen.

At the same time, this wasn't her. Gone were her black jean shorts and Doc Martens. The dark red lipstick that was nearly black. The smoky eyes that looked straight through me.

In its place was an elegant dress, a shade of white that

was almost cream, but not quite. I had never seen her in all white before. Her normally pale skin was tan from the afternoons we'd been spending in my pool and on the lake, so the color glowed against her skin rather than washing her out. Her blonde hair framed her round face, and those ice-blue eyes lit up at the sight of me. As if she'd just woken from a dream to find it was real.

She was the most beautiful thing I had ever seen in my entire life. There were no words for the way the light played along her face or the twinkle in her eye or the twist in my gut that said she was *mine*. Nothing else mattered.

So, I strode across the room and into the dim-lit bar, ignoring everything else in existence except my girl.

I swept her up into my arms. She laughed when I lifted her straight off her barstool, tossing her arms around my shoulders.

Then, I kissed her.

And I kissed her.

And I kissed her.

Like I could not last another second without her lips on me. Like I would die in the next breath if I couldn't have her.

I half-considered carrying her out of the bar just like that and home and into my bed, where she belonged. I had to physically pull back and remind myself that wasn't why I was here. Yes, I wanted to take her away from here, but I needed to make sure she first wanted to be saved. And then I needed to have a *word* with my sister.

I lowered Harley back to her feet.

Her breath came out in a soft pant as her eyes slowly opened. "Well, that is one way to say hello."

"What can I say? I missed you."

She shot me her mischievous grin. "Elsie told you, didn't she?"

"Elsie told me," I confirmed. "Why didn't *you* tell me?"

She shrugged. "It was no big deal."

"Really?" I asked in a disbelieving tone.

"If I keep saying it, it will be true."

I huffed. "I don't want you to have to deal with any unpleasantness from my family."

She laughed sharply. "What like a punch to the face?" She brushed my nose. "She's just trying to get a rise out of me. I'm not going to give it to her."

"I love you," I said and kissed her again.

Then, the rest of the world returned.

Kai had his arm around Elsie's shoulders, who was smirking at the two of us. "Um...PDA much?"

"You can't control them," Kai said with a shake of his head.

"They can't control themselves," Elsie said. "Get a room."

"Is that an option?" I asked.

"Oh my God, Chase," Ashleigh said, striding across the room.

I turned to my sister, doing a poor job of controlling the anger seething through me. And it was at the same moment, I noticed Kennedy. She was sipping a martini three stools down. Our eyes met briefly, and she held up her hands, as if to say, *I had nothing to do with this.* I hadn't seen her in a few years, but I believed her. She was already averting her gaze, slinking out of the picture, as if she could avoid the train wreck that she assumed was forthcoming.

"Ashleigh," I all but snarled.

Harley pinched me. "Play nice."

The last thing I wanted to do on this godforsaken earth was play nice with my sister.

"Brother of mine, what a surprise," she said cheerfully.

"Is it really?"

"You and Kai don't normally show up for our *girls' weekend*. There's *girls* in the title," she said with a laugh.

"Well, when I realized you were so close, I had to come and check on my girlfriend."

"And how did you find her?" she asked with that condescending smile.

"Enjoying my wine," Harley interrupted our showdown. "It's a Wright Vineyard red."

Ashleigh wrinkled her nose at the comment. Did Harley know that she had struck the perfect chord with Ashleigh? My sister had refused to ever try anything from the vineyard since Julian had dumped her.

"I prefer Sinclair Cellars," she said with a smile.

I cleared my throat. "Could you cut it out? I know what you're doing."

Ashleigh's eyes widened. "What do you mean?"

"Inviting Kennedy."

"Kennedy has an open invitation," Ashleigh argued.

"Fine. Then, inviting Harley when you knew my ex

would be here and then not warning either of us of the fact."

"Chase, it's fine," Harley said quickly.

"It's been *years*, Chase. I didn't even think about it. Why would any of that matter?"

Ashleigh was so good at playing dumb that I almost believed her. Except I knew her too well.

I took a step forward, putting myself between Ashleigh and Harley. I lowered my voice so that no one else could hear us. "I know you're still mad about Julian, but if you threaten my relationship again, it will be the last thing you do."

Her mouth popped open in surprise, and it was so satisfying. Until the look dropped off of her face and the warmth evaporated. "Don't *threaten* me, Chase. You're the one dating the *enemy* behind Dad's back."

"She is not the enemy."

"The *Wrights* are," she snapped. "And you know it."

"That's ridiculous. We've had it out with them, and it's old and tired. We need to move on."

"Just because you're fucking one of them doesn't change anything."

"It did for you."

She jerked back at my words. "Are you insane? Because I did everything I could do to bring Julian into the Sinclair fold."

"Look at how that worked out."

Ashleigh clenched her jaw. She knew it was the truth. Every wrong move she'd taken led to the destruction of her relationship. "So, if it's all in the past, why haven't you told Dad?"

"I plan to tell him."

She scoffed. "If you wanted to, you already would have."

"None of that fucking matters."

I stepped back away, fighting to regain control. Ashleigh had reeled me in. *Me*. Who knew every one of her games. I needed to stop. This would get us nowhere.

"None of that matters," I repeated more calmly. "Though I remember why I had reservations about this."

"Can't let your girlfriend off her leash?" she asked.

"Unlike you, I am not controlling what happens in everyone's life around me," I told her. "And I'm not putting up with this shit anymore." I wrapped an arm around Harley's waist. "Come on. Let's go home."

"Chase," Harley said, tugging on my arm. She scooted past me and smiled at my sister. "Ashleigh, this was really fun. Call me for next time."

Ashleigh's eyes widened with surprise. "Next time?"

"I mean, if you're paying for the spa again, then yes."

Elsie snorted a laugh behind us.

"Until next time," she said with a wave.

Ashleigh's shocked look was priceless.

11

———

HARLEY

My hands were shaking as I pushed out of the bar, through the double doors, and onto the sidewalk. That had not gone as planned. I'd thought I'd been holding it all in. But then Chase arrived and defended me. I hadn't even known I wanted that. I'd never needed it before, but now, I was bereft that, my entire life, I'd had to do all my own saving. And yes, I'd stood up to Ashleigh in the end, but only Chase's strength had helped me to walk out.

Kai and Elsie followed us out.

Kai chuckled under his breath. "Always a good time, Sinclair."

They shook hands as Elsie pulled me into a hug.

"Call me anytime, and we'll have our own girls' time, all right?"

"Thanks, Els."

I watched them walk away and followed Chase to the red Porsche parked on the street.

"Harley," he said as I reached the passenger side, "I know you're mad."

I turned and threw myself into his arms all at once. I pressed my lips to his. He groaned and tugged me in close, slanting our mouths together and taking me deeper.

"Well, hello," he murmured.

"I'm not mad."

"You're not?"

I shook my head. "Thanks for coming."

"Even though you didn't text me?"

"Yes."

"I had no idea Kennedy was going to be there. I never would have suggested that you go if…"

"Chase," I said with a laugh. "It's fine. I kind of gathered that you didn't know or else you wouldn't have burst in there like a knight in shining armor to rescue me."

"When you didn't need rescuing," he guessed.

"I was holding it down fine, but honestly, I wanted to leave."

I winced at the admission. I'd been trying to be a cool girl and just given up. That wasn't me, and it was nice to not have to spend another minute pretending.

He breathed out. "I'm glad I came then. When I saw that text, I just lost it."

"I noticed. Were you trying to get your sister to punch you?"

He threaded our fingers together. "I don't think clearly when it comes to you, I guess."

"Same. But what are you going to do about Ashleigh now?"

He sighed. "I don't know. I don't want to have to play these games."

"That seems to be her MO."

"It is."

"And...your dad?" I asked gently.

I understood viscerally why he didn't want to tell his dad. Aside from my mom, all of my family had found out when I didn't want them to. I'd never gotten to tell basically anyone about us without a huge scene.

"I'm going to tell him. I do *not* want Ashleigh to be the one to do it."

"Do you think she will?"

"I have no fucking clue," he admitted. "On some level, yes. On another, she'd want to save it for when it could hurt me the most—because that's how she functions."

"Christ, Chase."

"I know." He shook his head. "We're fucked up. I did mention that."

I laughed. "Well, if y'all are, then so are we."

"I'll try to work up the nerve sooner rather than later. Maybe I'll make dinner plans with him. Could we do dinner?"

"We can do dinner," I agreed.

He exhaled slowly. "All right. And again...I'm sorry I got you out of there."

"What? This is way better than dinner and more drinks with those girls. You were so right. I shouldn't have gone. That is not my scene." I pushed my hands up his chest, wrapping them around his neck. "I've never been comfortable with girls like that."

"I can't imagine you being uncomfortable in any situation."

"Oh no, I can *handle* myself," I said with a smirk, "but those girls know all the buttons to press."

"Like my ex." His head dropped down to rest against my forehead.

"Like your ex fiancée."

He winced. "I didn't purposely keep that information from you. I just...don't ever think about her."

I pulled back and looked up into his big blue eyes, the sincerity in every line, and just laughed. "Chase, did you think I was *jealous*?"

He shot me a sheepish look. "To be fair, I would be jealous of anyone who has ever looked at you."

"Okay, maybe I'm jealous of that," I answered honestly. "But I don't think I have anything to worry about."

"You don't," he rushed to assure me.

I pushed him backward gently. "You were basically single for three years because you were obsessed with me." I winked at him. "I know I have nothing to worry about."

"Oh, someone is *cocky* now, huh?" he asked, slipping his hands down the back of my cream dress.

"Should I not be?"

"It's fucking hot. So, please continue."

"Is this when I tell you that I want your cock?"

He nipped at my bottom lip. "Whenever you want it."

"Now?" I asked with a raised eyebrow as I grabbed for the handle on his Porsche.

"You've convinced me." He jogged around to the

driver's side and slipped in. "How exactly are we getting your car home?"

"Elsie dropped me off actually after she tried to persuade me not to go to the bar."

He laughed as he reversed out of his parking spot. "That sounds like Elsie. Guess she'd game-planned to have Kai and me meet you."

"I guess so."

My fingers were reaching for his pants. It was tricky in the car while he was maneuvering the stick shift, but I finally got his pants undone and the zipper down.

"Harley," he said as I palmed his cock, "I thought you meant when we got home."

"Should I stop?"

"Fuck."

His eyes fluttered as I dragged a nail down the shaft.

"Don't crash your very expensive car."

He managed a half-laugh. "Thanks for that suggestion."

I was just teasing him from the passenger seat, wanting nothing more than to slide over and get my mouth around him, but truly, there was no room. The car was tiny. My ass would probably be hanging out the window. Maybe that wouldn't be so bad. Not with the way he was looking at me as I put a little more pressure into my effort.

We hit a red light, and he grasped my wrist in his hand. "Harley."

"Should I stop?" I asked with no intention of doing so.

"I am...going to crash." His eyes met mine, hungry and desperate.

"Okay," I said, slowly extracting my hand with a feral grin.

"Oh no," he said.

"What?" I asked with faux innocence.

"I know that look. You're about to wreck my world."

I just grinned as my legs parted wide enough for him to get a good look. He groaned deep in the back of his throat. My hand went to my knee and skimmed down my inner thigh, stopping at the apex of my thighs. His eyes tracked me the whole way as I ran a finger up the front of my black thong and tipped my head back with a soft moan when I reached the bundle of nerves. His hand went to my knee, spreading me wider.

"What a fucking view, baby girl."

Honk.

We both jolted at the noise from the car behind us. The light had switched to green. He growled in frustration and gunned the car.

But I was far from done.

I slipped a finger under my thong and moved it to the side. "What about this view?"

He took a distracted peek as he shifted gears. "Fuck."

"A good fuck?" I asked as I strummed my clit gently, a little shiver running through me.

"Yes, you're going to get a good fuck as soon as we're home."

"Think I can come before then?"

His body tightened at those words. There was pained torture in his eyes when he stopped at the next light.

"You'd better fucking come." He leaned across the car, sliding two fingers into my awaiting pussy.

"Oh," I gasped.

I was still circling my clit, building that tension. But now, he was fucking my pussy hard, like he was clearly planning to do when we got home. We both waited on bated breath for the light to change. When his hand would need to shift gears and my pussy would once again be unoccupied.

"Fuck, you're so wet," he ground out.

"Green light," I gasped just as he curled his fingers up into me.

He swore under his breath and retreated. The Porsche lurched forward. I could see the speedometer lurch with it. He veered right off of the main drag and drove down side streets to avoid more lights. It didn't help because there were also ill-timed Stop signs, but we were moving faster at least.

"Didn't want to stop again?"

"I want to stop right the fuck now and fucking finish you off."

"Don't threaten me with a good time."

He arched an eyebrow. "That right?"

My hand was still between my legs. I was working up to that orgasm, imagining what it would be like when we got home after I finished.

Chase pulled over right in front of a stretch of abandoned buildings. We were still a solid five minutes from home, and by the look on his face, he'd given up on waiting that much longer.

"Chase," I whispered as he put the car in park.

"Spread wider," he demanded.

"Someone could see!"

His fingers slid back into me, returning to their previous speed. I shuddered all over.

"Then, you'd better be fast."

"I..." But I had no words left.

It was dusk. We were on the outskirts of downtown. Anyone could literally walk up and see me spread wide as he finger-fucked me. Still, I didn't stop.

"Come on, baby girl. I know you're close. I can feel that sweet cunt pulsing around my fingers."

My fingers trembled as I circled faster and faster and faster. His fingers pumped in and out of me. Our eyes locked in the small car. I held my breath as the world shattered. My orgasm hitting like a car crash. My body barely able to control itself as Chase slowed his strokes and milked it out of me.

"There you go," he soothed. "That's better."

It was my turn to say, "Fuck."

He chuckled softly. "Still promise to do that."

He removed his fingers while I was still coming down and pulled away. It was the fastest we ever got home. I was still in an orgasm-laced haze when he pulled into the driveway.

My feet barely hit the garage floor when he was there, throwing me over his shoulder. I shrieked in surprise. My ass half hanging out of my dress as he walked me across the living room and into his bedroom.

Chase shucked off his pants, stripped me of my thong, and a second later, thrust hard inside of me.

"Fucking hell. You're so goddamn wet."

"Your fault," I teased.

He grasped my wrists and positioned them above my head as he started a brutal pace. "*My* fault?"

I grinned. "You said I was cocky."

"If I'd known that was going to make you masturbate in the front seat of my Porsche, I would have called you that a lot sooner."

"I mean, I was going for road head."

He slowed to a downright painfully relaxed pace. My legs tightened around him, trying to get him to go fast again.

"You wanted to give me road head?"

"Probably not in the Porsche. Chase, please," I begged.

"No, tell me about this."

I groaned and tried to sit up, but he had me held in place as he stroked in and out of me at a leisurely pace. "How are you not dying to get off?"

"Tell me about road head."

"Fine. I want your cock in my mouth. I want the salty taste of your pre-come. I want the hard thrust of you into my throat because you can't fucking control yourself. I want to feel you shudder with desire as I deep-throat you. I want you to come down my throat and make a mess everywhere because I can barely take it all in. Then, I want you to fuck me until I can't think another thought." I shifted my hips temptingly. "Like right now."

"Well, now, I want that," he teased.

His eyes widened when my mouth opened. "Then, take it."

He didn't second-guess me, just slipped out of my

pussy and brought his slick, wet cock to my mouth. My hands came to his thighs as his came to the back of my head. I could taste my arousal on him. Then, there was no thought, just him fucking my mouth, in deep strokes that made me gag and choke. But he pulled back enough so I could breathe through it.

Then, in one long grunt, he thrust all the way back, emptying into my throat. I swallowed as much as I could, making a mess, just as I'd told him I would.

He watched me take down his come before burying his face in my pussy and taking me easily over the edge a second time. I came so hard that I screamed and tried to push his head away because I was so sensitive. But he wouldn't let me. Just rode my face for dear life as I crested.

We both collapsed back on the bed after.

He threaded our fingers together, bringing my hand up to his lips and pressing a kiss there. "You're magnificent."

"Mmm," I agreed.

He rolled over to me and stroked my hair for so long that I nearly fell asleep before I heard him ask, "Was it all worth it?"

"What?"

"Today with my sister?"

"The spa was great. Plus, I got orgasms at the end."

"Bonus-gasms."

I snorted. "Oh my God, bonus-gasms."

"I'll give you as many as you want."

I ducked my head into his shoulder and whispered, "Chase."

"Hmm?"

"Go to West's wedding with me."

He froze with his fingers in my hair. "Look at me."

I pulled back to meet his eyes. "Do you not want to go? I know my family—"

"Fuck our families. You're mine, right?"

I nodded.

"Then, I'm going."

"In front of all the Wrights?"

"Every one of them, baby girl. Every single one of them."

12

CHASE

I n theory, agreeing to a Wright wedding was a good idea.

In practice...

Well, this was a whole other adventure.

"Stop acting nervous," Harley said. Her fingers moved to the knot at my throat. She straightened it out. "It's going to be fine."

"I'm not nervous."

She coughed around a laugh. "Yeah, okay."

Her hands splayed down the front of the suit I was wearing for Weston and Nora's wedding. It was a huge, elaborate affair at Wright Vineyard, the place where Harley and I had first met. Only a different brother was getting married now.

We were in the cellar, where all the girls were getting ready for the event. Hair and makeup and mimosas, oh my!

"Stop looking at me like that, too," she said, smacking my chest playfully.

"Like what?"

"You know. I already feel ridiculous."

She slipped her hands down the shimmery confection dress. It was a floor-length rose-gold number that fell off of her shoulders with a sweetheart neck. Her platinum hair was pinned off of her face, and her makeup was neutral and stunning, highlighting her round face, the dimple in her bottom lip, and wide eyes.

But it was not black.

She wasn't even in her customary Doc Martens. Through the thigh-high slit, real high heels were visible, elevating her a solid four inches. Still not quite eye level with me but closer.

"You look stunning."

"It's *rose gold*," she grumbled.

"Beautiful in and out of everything."

"At least I have a tan." Which she'd gotten from our hours out on the lake and in my swimming pool. Then, she shivered. "Never thought I'd say that."

"My pasty queen."

She shot me a look, and I grinned, tugging her in for a kiss.

A throat cleared behind us. We broke away quickly and turned to find Eve standing at the door.

"As adorable as this is," Eve said, gesturing to us, "probably don't let the boys see it."

"They can deal," Harley said.

"Noted," I said instead. Harley gave me a disbelieving look. "Hey, it's West's wedding."

"Fine." She held her hands up. "Look, I can keep my

hands to myself." She glanced back at me with a look that promised she wouldn't later.

Eve must have noticed because she snorted. "All right. Come on, Harley. It's almost time. We'll see you out there, Chase."

I waved good-bye as Eve tugged Harley back to the bridal suite. Music was coming from the vineyard grounds, where hundreds of chairs had been set up for practically the entire town. The Wrights were beloved, of course. But Nora was an Abbey, which was the other half of the vineyard family with Jordan and Julian. Not to mention, she had a successful wedding planning business of her own. And even more than that, West was a member of one of the biggest bands in the world. So, half of LA had shown up in their sleek outfits and spray tans. It was a spectacle.

I was hoping that would mean that *I* wouldn't be one.

And I was *wrong*.

Somehow, three-plus years later, there were still whispers following me.

I ignored them as I strode down that aisle and took my seat with a perfect view of where my girl would be standing in the line of bridesmaids.

What else could I do?

A Sinclair at a Wright wedding.

Luckily, the moment lasted only as long as the music shift. The crowd turned to find Harley leading the bridesmaids down the aisle. She stood tall and proud, the rose-gold dress shimmering in the late afternoon summer sun. She was a vision. And though five other bridesmaids trailed after her, all her friends and family, my eyes were only for her.

She took her place at the end of the flower-covered altar. Once she turned to face the crowd, flowers in her hands, her eyes sought me out. Then and only then, her eyes crinkled into a smile, and her shoulders dropped.

I winked at her, and a flush came to her cheeks.

My girl.

And I was here for her. No matter what any of the other Wrights thought about my presence or our relationship. I was showing up. I was this serious.

"Introducing Weston and Nora Wright!"

I applauded with the rest of the crowd as the barn doors opened and in strode the entirety of the bridal party. West and Nora at the center of the group, who shocked everyone by changing out of the huge princess-cut dress and into a knee-length number and white cowboy boots. Two dresses for one bride.

And she wasn't the only one who had changed.

I laughed as soon as I saw Harley, who had clearly taken her floor-length dress off above the knees and switched to her Docs. I cheered louder, my eyes on Harley, and Nora twirled in place for the crowd. But Harley ran straight for me.

I picked her up around the waist and spun her. All eyes were on her brother and his new wife anyway. For a moment, we were transported back in time to that night at Jordan and Annie's wedding. Just the two of us in a crowded room, wanting nothing but to find an escape. And we'd found one in each other.

"Look at your dress," I said as she slid down my front and back to her feet.

"Like it?"

"I love it."

"Everyone thought I was nuts at first, but when Blaire was finished cutting, they approved. I still think Nora doesn't like the shoes." She kicked up one clunky Doc Marten. "Oh well."

"Oh well indeed." My hand went to the necklace around her neck. The *H* Tiffany's necklace that I'd given to her for her birthday all those years ago. "And this?"

"You like?"

"You know I do."

"Good. Because it's my fav." Harley took my hand. "Come on." She dragged me to the front of the crowd to watch West and Nora dance.

I could admit that West could move. Not to mention, he and Nora seemed to perfectly fit. I was happy for them. It was an interesting thing to recognize. Not that I'd been against them in particular, but how, over the last couple of years, things had changed enough that I didn't just loathe the thought of happiness for the Wrights.

I had my own Wright who I wanted to keep happy after all.

The dance ended, and Nora encouraged everyone to come out and have one more dance with them. Harley dragged me onto the floor in front of everyone.

"You're the one who knows how to dance," she reminded me.

Ah yes, years of dances I was forced to attend for the Junior League had taught me how to twirl a girl around. So, I gave her what she wanted, tugging her close and leading her around the room effortlessly. Harley's eyes were wide with wonder, as if she'd forgotten just how capable I was at this or maybe it was just a whole different experience now that we were a couple.

"What are you thinking?" I asked.

"This is like a redo."

"Almost."

"Almost?"

"Well, this time, you're already mine." I spun her out away from me, her eyes shining, her smile wide. Then, I whipped her back in. I kissed the tip of her nose. "I'm not just meeting and getting to know the girl of my dreams."

"You're right. This is better."

"Much," I agreed.

The music came to a close, and as I had the first time, I dipped Harley dramatically to the ground. She laughed the whole way down, dropping her head back. Then, when she looked up at me again, I kissed her, right there in front of everyone.

I lost myself in that kiss. It was easy with Harley to forget that anyone else was around. To forget the rest of the world even existed.

But as I pulled her back to her feet, the entire world crashed back together.

Because Harley's four brothers were striding toward us.

My hackles went up. Even when I told myself that in no way were they going to cause a scene at West's wedding. Nora would murder him before letting him do that. The rest of the girls would certainly intercede. And yet they were still approaching.

Harley took my hand and stood her ground as they stopped in front of us. My heart was pounding. I didn't know whether I was going to get reprimanded or punched.

What was happening here? How did I keep it from hurting Harley? Because I was done letting anyone else hurt her.

"Sinclair," Jordan said.

"Wright," I said with a nod in his direction.

Then, after a long silence, Jordan stuck his hand out. Just as he had at that soccer game where Harley was injured.

The relief must have shown on my face as I put my hand in his and shook perhaps a little harder than necessary. Jordan smirked.

"Scared you?" he asked.

"Don't be an ass," Harley said, swatting at Jordan. Then, she threw herself into West's arms. "Married! You're married!"

He laughed, hugging her back. "Thanks, sis."

I shook Julian's hand next.

"Glad you're making her happy."

"That's all I want."

"She told me what happened with Ashleigh."

I winced. "I didn't know that was going to happen."

Julian laughed. "Don't I, of all people, know what Ashleigh is capable of?"

"Fair," I said, defensive despite my own frustration at my sister.

"But you seem chill, man." Julian patted my shoulder.

My shoulders dropped again. He wasn't saying my whole family was like Ashleigh. That we were all terrible. He was...accepting me with Harley.

Whitt was next, putting his hand out. "I didn't want to like you."

"The feeling was mutual," I said with a laugh.

"And I'll still destroy you if you hurt her."

"Fair," I interjected. "I'm not planning to hurt her."

Whitt nodded. "Good."

And that was enough.

West punched me playfully in the arm. "That's for the one I missed the first time."

I snorted. "Thanks, man."

"Glad you could come to the wedding. Dude, let's go eat some fucking food. I'm starving."

Then, he had his arm around his new pixie wife, and away we went. The night was a whirlwind of food and dancing and cake and traditional wedding things. At the start of the bouquet toss, I grasped Harley's hand firmly and gestured toward the exit.

Her eyes widened, and she nodded eagerly.

Without a backward glance, we slipped out of the party. Night had fully fallen, and the stars were bright out in this rural part of Lubbock. The vineyards were large and looming to the left of us on the pathway between the barn and cellar. The world was at our fingertips. Like we could pluck the stars out of the heavens for our entertainment.

"So," Harley said with a smirk, "what kind of music do you like?"

I laughed and linked our fingers together. "Big fan of David Bowie."

"Oh my God, do you know I always wanted to name a dog Bowie?"

"What a happy coincidence. I have a dog named Bowie."

"Stop!" she said with a gasp. "We're fated."

"Fated," I agreed.

We continued leisurely down the path and into the winding vineyards. We were the only ones out here. I was glad that we got to redo this moment. To have every perfect part re-created the same, but different. Better.

We stopped at a bench in the vineyard, completely secluded from even the noise of the party. She wrapped her arms around my neck. Her eyes nearly silver in the moonlight. So open, so trusting. All mine.

I slid my hands down her legs and hoisted her up into my arms. She wrapped her legs around my waist. Then, her mouth descended, capturing a perfect kiss.

"I'll tell you a secret if you tell me one of your own," I whispered against her lips.

"I have a scar on my hip from ice skating."

"I have one on my eyebrow from kayaking." I kissed her again. "Trade me another."

"I'm in love with my family's enemy who is way too old for me."

I chuckled softly. "I'm in love with my family's enemy who is *way* too young for me." My hands slipped up to her ass. "Trade me one more."

She pulled back just enough to meet my gaze. "Being with you terrifies me."

I blinked in surprise. "Why is that?"

"Because there's nothing I want more in the entire world and I'd watch it all burn to keep this."

My heart stuttered at her honesty.

She bit her lip. "Your secret?"

So, I gave her the truth.

"I feel like I can't breathe when I'm with you," I whispered like an admission. "Like everything is so fucking good and so fucking real. That I don't know how I went a single minute of my life without you in it. Sometimes, I pause and wonder how I got this lucky and how everyone else can't see it and how I don't fucking care because I feel it in every inch of my body."

She didn't balk at my honesty. She didn't look like she was ready to run. She looked a hundred and ten percent in this. As much as I was.

"Chase," she pleaded.

It was all the motivation I needed before laying her out on that bench and laying claim to her body, mind, and soul.

She gasped at the first thrust as I moved inside of her, but she never closed her eyes. She looked directly at me, saw every piece of me, and accepted me for who I was. She wanted this. I wanted this. I would fight to keep it at any cost.

Our body thumped together rhythmically. The only sound other than our heavy breathing. Her fingers traced my jawline before pulling me in for another kiss. A silent promise of her affection. The love that had developed and sharpened to a razor's edge. And I felt all of it.

As we pushed to climax, everything shattered, dissolving into starlight and reforming into this union. With the woman that I loved with my entire fucking heart.

PART III

BLUFF

13

—————

HARLEY

"I have an idea," Chase said as we sat in his Porsche.

I reached across the stick shift and took his hand. "Is it that we don't go to dinner?"

He grimaced. "You read me so easily."

"You've been dreading this all week."

"Haven't you?"

I shrugged. Yes, of course I'd been anxious about what was to come, but I didn't want Chase to see it. Not if I could help it.

"I mean...is it that bad of an idea?"

"It's the best idea," I agreed. "But we can't."

Chase sighed and started the engine. "I know."

After the wedding, Chase had been good to his word. He'd scheduled dinner with his dad. Ashleigh hadn't told him about us. Chase would get to be the one to do it. Not that he *wanted* to be the one to do it. In fact, some part of me wondered if he was hoping that Ashleigh would just spill the news so it'd all be out there. I was sure he didn't actually want that, but equally sure he didn't really want his father to know at all.

I couldn't blame him. I felt the same about my dad, and I didn't work with him every day. Holding it in day in and day out must have been torture.

"Are you worried about me being there?"

Chase pulled out of the driveway and veered south toward his father's house. "I'm worried about it all."

"You could go by yourself?" I offered.

"Do you not want to meet my dad?" he asked in a teasing voice.

"Would you blame me?"

"Not at all. He's an ass." He sighed and stopped at the Stop sign. His eyes found mine. "You don't have to go if you don't want to."

"No, I'm not backing out. I was trying to give you an option for whatever made this easier for you. You were there for me when everyone on my side found out. You don't have to do this alone."

"Yet you're sticking that bottom lip out," he said, leaning over and sucking it between his teeth. "The pout is too cute."

"I'm not pouting," I said, dragging him deeper into a kiss.

His laugh was a rumble. "I'll turn around. We can stay home. I can order in Chinese."

"No way. Not after what happened with my family."

"You're sure?"

"I'm sure."

He nodded and continued driving. "I'd understand, you know? I probably should have just told him at work this morning, but I didn't want to deal with it at the office. So I'd told him I had a girlfriend, but not that you're a Wright. Am I a coward?"

"No, you shouldn't have to deal with any of this," I said with a frustrated sigh. I twiddled the *H* necklace he'd given me so long ago around my finger. "It shouldn't even be a big deal."

"Everything with us is a big deal. Wrights and Sinclairs don't mix."

"Yeah," I muttered. "Unfortunately."

"If your family can come around, then so can mine."

"Are we sure my family has officially come around?"

Chase shrugged. "Probably not, but they're working on it."

"Then, that'll happen with your dad, too."

"Here's to hoping."

Chase flipped on the radio, and Queen blared through the speakers. We sang along together, forgetting the impending doom of his father on the horizon. It was just us living our best life. This was all I'd wanted with Chase for so long when we were apart. This moment right here.

It was over too soon as Chase pulled into the gated community on the south side of town. In a place like Lubbock, there weren't very many gated areas. Most people didn't have anything to hide behind their gates, but of course, his dad lived in one. The place was a total McMansion. Two stories with tiered balconies and a circle drive behind another gate with a four-car garage. There was an inner courtyard as well as at least an acre fenced in. I could peek a pergola and swimming pool in the backyard.

"Whoa," I muttered.

"Yeah. It's a lot."

"You grew up here?"

He nodded. "My dad had the house built when I was a kid. It's like a fortress."

"Hmm," I said softly. "Looks more foreboding than welcoming."

"That's the point."

Chase pulled the Porsche through the second gate and into the giant drive. He parked before one of the many garages and cut the engine.

"Not too late to bail."

"I think it is," I said, taking his hand and pressing a kiss to his knuckles. "We can do this."

"Yeah. You're right."

We got out of the car, and for a second, my breath caught at the sight of him. He was wearing a gray suit coat over a sky-blue button-up and khaki slacks. The Rolex on his wrist was briefly visible as he buttoned the top of his coat. His dirty-blond hair had been styled, and I could smell the scent of his favorite cologne. And though I loved every inch of what I saw, I knew how much of his appearance tonight was nerves.

He was more than comfortable in a suit. I'd never seen one wear him and not the other way around. But tonight, it was close, only because he fidgeted with the length at his wrists and adjusted the collar. I could practically see him wondering if he should have worn a tie.

We were so similar in so many ways. Our fathers were

unfortunately one of them. I was glad that Owen was out of my life. That he didn't have a way to make me this nervous or impact my relationship anymore. I wanted that for Chase, but with the company still controlled by his father, there were still strings attached.

If I could cut them for him, then I would.

Instead, I stood in a little black dress, doing my best to walk the path with him.

"Ready?" he asked.

He turned back to face me, holding his hand out. The other held a bottle of wine. I'd chosen it based on my mom's favorite vineyard in Willamette Valley. I'd thought it would be better than bringing something local with all the tension we were trying to avoid. This was more of a peace offering.

"Are you?"

"As ready as I'll ever be."

I took his hand, and he tucked me into his side. That was going to have to be good enough.

We walked up the entranceway that led to the enormous front door. It had double wrought iron doors, each larger than a regular door. It was as if we'd shown up at the Beast's castle, trying to rescue someone from the dungeons.

I gulped as Chase rang the doorbell. He squeezed my hand for reassurance.

A minute later, the door pulled open, and a young woman stood on the threshold. She was a stunner. Petite and lithe, like she lived in a ballet class, with classic blonde hair and a narrow face. Her makeup was picture-perfect with neutral lipstick, and she had freshly painted red-lacquered nails. She wore a cream designer dress and nude heels. The spitting image of a trophy housewife.

Except there was no ring on her finger.

Arnold refused to make it official. Despite his late-twenties mistress giving him a child.

"Y'all made it!" Dayna said with a smile.

"Hello, Dayna," Chase said formally.

He'd mastered the wince that I could feel under the surface. Under other circumstances, this girl could have been going after him, but somehow, she was with a man twice her age.

"Come on in. Dinner is almost finished. Arnold should be out any minute."

I followed Chase inside, wishing that I were the one holding the wine. So that I'd have something to do with my hands.

"You must be Chase's new girlfriend." Dayna held her hand out. "I'm Dayna. It's so nice to meet you."

"Harley," I said, shaking her hand.

"So glad to have both of you over. I know Arnold is as well."

Chase covered a scoff with a cough. Then, he thrust the bottle of wine toward Dayna. "We brought you this."

"That's so thoughtful," she said. "I'm more of a white wine drinker, but this looks amazing."

"It's my favorite," I offered. "I used to drink it with my mom all the time."

"Well then, I will have to try it. Arnold prefers red anyway."

A battle cry rang out from the upstairs, and

suddenly, a little kid was throwing his body down the stairs at full speed. Dayna giggled as her son vaulted toward her.

"Silas, baby, what are you doing? Mommy and Daddy have plans. We talked about this. You're with the nanny tonight."

"Mama!" he cried, throwing himself on the ground.

She flushed at his behavior and apologized to us. "Sorry about this. He's such a mommy's boy."

"No need to apologize," I said automatically.

"Always want to see my little brother anyway."

Chase beamed at the kid. In every way, he should loathe how this child had come to be. His father had ruined their family, and this little boy was the result. But it wasn't his fault after all. He was the innocent in all of this. And Chase said he was a sweet little boy. So unlike their father, which was probably more indicative of who was actually raising him.

"Chase!" Silas cried, abandoning his mother for his brother.

Chase hauled him up around the middle and swung him in a circle. "Little man."

"You're going to get him all riled up," Dayna said, but with no bite. She was smiling. Her eyes alight at the sight of them. Almost a look like she wished *this* were her life and Chase wasn't her little boy's brother, but father instead.

"Tell me all about what's been going on," Chase said.

The little boy began to speak in incoherent babbles while waving his hand animatedly. I only caught every fifth word, but Chase and Dayna hung on to every single thing he said. Like they knew the shape of all of his words, even when they weren't exactly intelligible.

"Okay. Okay. Go back upstairs," Dayna said. "You can spend time with Chase later."

"Have to?" he asked with a pout.

"Yes, up you go."

She gently patted his butt, and he hurried back up the stairs, waving at us as he went.

"Sorry again."

"It's good to see him," Chase said.

"He's the joy of my life," Dayna said. "It's good that you spend time with him. He needs it." She smiled sadly again and then forced those emotions away. "Let's open this up."

She hoisted the wine up and herded us toward the dining room. We had just crossed out of the living room when Arnold Sinclair stepped out of what I imagined was the master bedroom.

He was an imposing man. Thick around the middle with thinning hair and a sour expression. I'd never understand why women threw themselves at him, but money made fools of so many. Plus, he had to be charming. Even if he was currently looking at all of us as if he'd just sucked a particularly tart lemon.

"What the *fuck* is a Wright doing in my house?" he snapped.

14

CHASE

Here we go.

"Dad, I want to introduce you to my girl-friend, Harley."

He looked between me and Harley and back, as if he couldn't quite believe the words that had just come out of my mouth.

I'd told him at work that I was seeing someone.

That it was serious.

That I was in love.

And that I wanted him to meet her.

He'd joked with me. Delighted that I was finally settling down. He'd been so happy at the prospect. Like I was becoming the man he wanted me to be. Even if that was an absurd idea. I didn't want to be my dad. Not when I saw what he was like with everyone else. Me, my mom, Ashleigh, Dayna, Silas. We were all just collateral damage. I had no doubt that he'd ditch Dayna and his son as soon as he found someone younger.

"No," was my dad's only reply.

"Arnold, they brought us wine," Dayna said, holding up the bottle.

"Trash it," he snarled.

Her eyes rounded. "It's a red, just like you like it."

But he wasn't even looking at her. This girlfriend that was playing trophy wife. She was nothing to him in that moment.

Fuck.

Maybe I'd underestimated my father. I'd thought he would keep it together long enough to have dinner. That he wouldn't be happy, but he'd lay it out on me after we left. He did not look like he was going to do that now. He was a volcano on the verge of erupting and burning everything in his path.

"We don't have to do this," I said quickly. If I could mitigate the fall out, I'd do it.

"You bring *her* here, to my house, and tell me we don't have to do it."

"We don't."

My father shot me an *are you an idiot* look. "What did you think was going to happen?"

"I thought you were going to meet my girlfriend," I snapped.

His eyes swiveled to Harley, who stood defiantly at my side. Her chin was lifted. I knew that look on her face. *Fuck around and find out.* She'd used it with her own father. She wasn't about to back down from mine.

"Your girlfriend." He repeated the words like they were disgusting.

"That's me," Harley said.

Dayna cleared her throat. "Maybe we should just open the wine, Arnold."

He ignored her again as he strode across the room to stand before Harley. Every instinct told me to get between them. My danger signs were firing rapidly. It took everything in me not to put her behind me or just walk out of that room. Maybe it would have been smarter to do that, knowing my father.

"So, you're the new one," he said flippantly.

"That's me," she repeated.

"I hope you realize this is just a rebellion."

Harley looked dubious. "He's in his thirties. Isn't that what teenagers do?"

"I suppose you'd know," he muttered.

She arched an eyebrow. "We're really not here to be insulted. So, if that's the best that you have, then can we move on and eat some dinner?"

"Yes, let's listen to Harley," I said confidently, sliding my arm across her shoulders. "Dinner, Dad?"

He was going to give. I could see it in the set of his shoulders. He wanted to be happy for me. He wanted to have dinner with me. Especially with how distant we'd been after the divorce. I had known he wanted to reconcile and used that to my advantage.

Then, the tension returned, and my hope dissolved.

"No Wright is sitting at my table."

"Arnold," Dayna said.

"Shut the fuck up, Dayna," he snarled. "This has nothing to do with you."

She curved in on herself, pulling the wine into her body. "Oh," she whispered. "I'll just..."

Then, she sniffled and disappeared into the kitchen.

Harley took a step toward her as if she could fix the fragile thing that my dad had broken. "Don't speak to her that way."

"I will speak to her however I see fit." He lifted himself to his height. "Who the fuck are you to be critical of me in my own house?"

"Dad," I warned.

Why hadn't I realized that putting oil and water in the room wasn't going to work out? Harley never backed down from a fight, and she had a problem with male authority figures. With good reason, to be fair, but she wasn't going to let this go. Not after he yelled at Dayna.

She glanced up at me. I could see the fire in her eyes. She wanted to slowly dress him down until he paid for all the shit that he'd done to all of those in his path over the years. She could do it. But it would also burn a bridge that there'd be no coming back from.

She ground her teeth together. A moment of growth, watching her not give in to my father's bullshit. "I should check on Dayna."

"She's fine," he snapped.

Harley looked up at me with concern in her eyes. She did not want Dayna to be alone right now. Not after the way my dad was. But he was blocking her path. I shook my head slightly. Even though I hated it.

"You can drop the act," my dad said.

We both looked up at him again. I had no idea if there was a way to salvage this, but I needed to try.

"Dad, we did this in good faith. We're together. There's no act."

He chuckled, a disbelieving sound. "No, you've never been a good actor," he said to me. "It's here." He pointed a meaty finger at Harley. "She's twisted your mind."

Harley's eyes rounded. "What?"

"Don't think I don't know who your father is."

Harley's back went ramrod straight. She clamped her mouth shut to keep from speaking venom against her old man.

"Her dad has nothing to do with this. Can we just have a civil conversation?"

But he wasn't listening to me. He wasn't even looking at me.

"Owen Wright is a manipulative, conniving snake," he spat. "He's the kind of man who will do anything to get what he wants, to ruin his enemies. And what are we? Sinclairs and Wrights have *always* been enemies. This is some kind of bullshit, twisted game that you're playing." His eyes narrowed. "And you're just fucking like him."

Harley took a step back at the vitriol. I couldn't think of a worse insult that he could have uttered in her presence. Owen Wright was her greatest fear. The last thing she wanted in the entire world was to be like him. Fuck.

I physically put myself between my dad and Harley.

"That is *enough*," I growled. "You will *not* speak to her like that. I don't care whose house this is. None of what you said is true. This was a mistake."

My dad opened his mouth, but I'd already turned, putting my back to my old man.

I took Harley's hand in my own and pressed a kiss to her knuckles. "Are you okay?"

She was shaking with anger. She opened and closed

her mouth, as if the very thought of speech might cause her to explode.

"Why don't you give us a minute? You can wait in the car."

She nodded. "That's probably for the best."

I offered her the keys. "Turn Bowie on and decompress."

A ghost of a smile touched her lips. "You know me so well."

She took the keys and disappeared through the door. I waited until the door clicked shut behind her before I turned to face my father.

A tic in my jaw was the only indication that I could barely hold myself back from decking him. I'd been punched by Wrights twice, and I'd never been as offended as the way my father—a grown-ass man—had just treated my girlfriend. I'd known it wasn't going to be perfect. I hadn't imagined whatever the fuck this was.

"You're going to side with a Wright over me," my dad said.

I laughed. I honestly couldn't help it. Even knowing it was going to set him off. "Do you hear yourself? You *ruined* our family so long ago. You cheated on Mom time and time again. You got another girl pregnant while you were married. The board pushed you out of the public eye to hide what you'd done. I don't understand how you think you have a single leg to stand on here. I brought Harley to you out of good faith. I wanted you to meet her, and instead, you insulted her." I shook my head. "I don't know why I even bothered."

"None of that has anything to do with what you're doing."

"If you believe that, then you're delusional."

My dad crossed his arms. "So, we're going to ignore the fact that she looks like a teenager. You're coming after me, and yet like father, like son."

I had no words for that. How I'd spent so long without the girl of my dreams to not be like my dad. And he was still throwing it in my face.

"I'm not here to argue about Harley. You wouldn't be throwing that at me if you thought the fact that you're dating women half your age was okay," I snapped back at him.

His nostrils flared. "You're going to judge me? With that girl in your bed?"

"That girl is a woman in her twenties. I wasn't *married*," I yelled back. "I didn't have *kids*. I didn't have a *life* with someone else. Don't you dare compare Harley to what you did."

"You can't be with her," he said instead.

I blinked. "You have no control over that."

"I'll disinherit you," he threatened. "I'll give it all to Silas."

I saw red at the suggestion. I didn't fucking care about the money, but the very idea that he could strong-arm me with *money* was absurd.

"Fine," I snarled. "Do it! For all I fucking care, Dad. I'm done with this conversation."

I turned and headed toward the door, but he followed on my heels.

"Don't you dare turn your back on me!"

"Why not?" I called over my shoulder. "You turned your back on all of us long ago."

"You can't be with a Wright," he yelled at me, spittle leaving his mouth as he came fully to his fury. "If you don't care about the money, then maybe you'll care about your job."

"Is that a threat?" I clenched my hands into fists.

"You can't work at Sinclair while you're with a Wright."

"Watch me."

"I'll fire you myself."

"No need," I shot back. Wrenching the door open, I threw over my shoulder, "I quit!"

15

HARLEY

Chase dropped into the driver's seat. His cheeks were blotchy, and I could see fire behind his eyes. Whatever had happened when I left hadn't made anything better. If anything, it had made it all worse.

Well, so much for hoping this would go better than my family.

His father was unstable. His anger over the feud between our families had physically altered his brain. I still couldn't believe that he'd fucking accused me of being like Owen. The fucking audacity.

It had only been by sheer force of will that I didn't unleash on him. If I'd thought that it would be any good, then I would have done so. I could have shown him exactly how like Owen I could be when pushed. He'd been the one to teach me how to argue after all. I could debate with the best of them.

But the lesson here had been when to back down. What good would any of it have done? He wasn't going to change his mind about me or my family. And he certainly hadn't changed my mind about him.

Chase silently stewed as he pulled out of the gated house through the gated community and back to his house. Bowie was still playing at full volume when he parked in the garage.

When he killed the engine, the sudden silence was unbearable.

"What a fucking asshole," I exploded.

Chase nodded. "Yep."

He opened the door, and I followed him into the house. I tossed my purse on the table. I just wanted to rage. The whole thing had been bullshit.

We should have seen it coming. Maybe we'd known it would be bad. But I certainly hadn't expected this.

"Maybe we should have just let Ashleigh tell him," I said as I went to the record player and chose an AC/DC album at random.

"I should have just told him at the office."

He disappeared into the bedroom to let Bowie out. The dog bounded out after us and then through the new doggie door. At least someone was happy.

"Probably, but then you would have had this happen at work. That wouldn't have been ideal."

"No," he agreed.

He leaned back against the back of the couch and crossed his arms. I didn't know how he was so calm. But of course, he wasn't the one who had been told he was like the person he hated most in the world. At least as far as I knew.

"I'm sorry about what he said to you."

"Yeah, fuck him."

"Perfectly reasonable response," Chase said softly.

"I mean, I know he's your father, but I can't believe you still talk to him after all this shit. You *saw* how he treats Dayna. He's never going to raise Silas. I don't even know what he cares about."

"Status," he said.

"And you have to *work* with him."

Chase cleared his throat. "About that."

I turned around in confusion and realized that I hadn't been reading him right at all. I'd thought he was furious like I was. But apparently, I had been projecting my anger onto him.

No, he was mad. But he was also...somber. Maybe a little freaked out.

He was slumped forward, his hands laced together over one knee. His eyes locked on his hands.

What the fuck was going on?

"About what?"

"I don't have to worry about that anymore."

"What does that mean?"

He coughed and then met my gaze. "I quit."

"*Excuse me*?" I gasped.

"I quit my job."

I stared at him, slack-jawed. Those could *not* have been the words that came out of his mouth. I must have misheard him. But he'd repeated them. He had said them twice. And still, it didn't compute.

"You can't quit your job."

"Yeah. Well, turns out, I can."

"Chase," I said slowly, as if I were approaching someone who was a flight risk, "you *can't* quit your job."

He crossed his arms. "I don't know what you expected me to do. He was being irrational. He insulted you. He threatened to disinherit me."

"He did what?"

"He thought he could win any argument, and I refused to play his game."

"That's fine, but that doesn't mean you *quit* your job," I reiterated.

"It's already done, Harley. I don't think you're hearing me. It's over."

I took a step back. "Chase, are *you* hearing yourself? You love your job. You've been putting up with your dad for literal years because you've always wanted to run the company."

"Yeah, well, I guess that's over."

"What? Why? Because he was a dick?" I gasped, completely flabbergasted by this answer.

He jumped to his feet and gestured to me. "He doesn't get to dictate this relationship. He doesn't get to insult you and get away with it."

"Wait," I said horrified, holding up a hand. "Are you saying that you quit because of *me*?"

"I mean, partially," he admitted. "He said that I couldn't have my inheritance if I was with a Wright. That I couldn't work at the company if I was dating a Wright."

The bottom dropped out of my stomach. "So, you quit."

"Yes."

I shook my head and took another step backward.

Oh no. Oh no, no, no. I couldn't handle this. This could not be happening.

"You can't quit because of me."

"Fine. I quit because of him," he said with a shrug. "Who fucking cares why I did it? It's over. I'll go back to the law firm or whatever. It's fucking fine." He stomped across the room, running his hand back through his hair and making it perfectly clear that it was *not* fucking fine.

"No," I said.

He whipped around. "What do you mean, no?"

"I mean, *no*, Chase. No, you're not quitting because of me. If that's what you want, fine, but I know it's not."

"Well, it happened," he snarled.

I reared back at the anger in his voice. "Watch your tone. I am not the bad guy here."

He closed his eyes and walked away from me. "You don't understand my father."

"I thought I was one of the few people who could perfectly understand the fucked up situation you're in with your dad."

"You went no contact years ago," he argued, throwing a hand in my direction. "You gave up. You don't have to deal with Owen. You haven't been pandering to him for years. You said fuck it, and it was done."

"Is that what you think? I made a deal with Owen for law school for *you*. Look at how well that worked out. Shouldn't that be everything you need to know about making the same deal with your dad?"

"I'm *not* making the same deal," he argued. "I'm making the opposite. I'm saying enough is enough. I've put in my time. It's irreconcilable. I cannot work with him every day anymore. Not if he wants to play games with my relationship."

"So, you're going to give up on your dream for me?"

"That's not—"

"It is," I snapped. "That is *exactly* what's happening."

"Harley."

He reached for me, and I backed up. I loved him. I loved him so much. But I could not deal with this right now. I couldn't be the scapegoat to his anger with his dad. I wasn't going to be the *reason* for any of this. He'd have to confront it for what it really was eventually. And if I was the reason, then we had a bigger problem in our relationship.

His hand dropped, and he looked hurt at my retreat. "Why are you so mad about this?"

"The fact that you don't know is telling."

He frowned. "Don't do that. Don't act like I should be able to read your mind."

"I always thought you could before," I said softly.

"Normally, we are on the same page."

"Yeah."

He ground his teeth together. "I thought you'd be pleased that I didn't give in to my dad."

"Chase, I hate your dad. I hate my dad. I want them to both suffer. What I don't want is for you to make decisions without me." I sighed. "I thought that was the point of being together. We were going to do this together."

"We *are* doing this together. That's why I brought you to meet my dad."

"And now, you're *quitting your job* because of *me*. Don't you remember when I got into Harvard?"

"What does that have to do with this?"

"You told me to take you out of the situation. To look at Harvard without you or my dad or anything. Did I want it? Was this how I wanted things to go? You said it was too important for me to decide that I wanted to stay in Lubbock for you. I needed to decide what I actually wanted."

"Yeah but—"

"This is just as important."

"I mean, of course I want to work at the company. That's what I've worked toward my whole life." He crossed his arms. "But I can't do it under his stipulations. I'm not giving you up for that."

I took a deep breath. He was still too upset to see what was right in front of him, and I wasn't getting through to him. I wanted to stay. I wanted to talk all of this out. I probably could. I could bang my head against the wall until we were both blue in the face, but he wouldn't see what I was saying.

"You're going to regret it, and you're going to blame me," I told him, throwing his words back in his face.

He winced at the words. "So be it."

I closed my eyes at those words. That wasn't going to work for me. I'd wanted to be with Chase for so long. The last couple of months had felt like a fever dream. So much Chase time. Everything was perfect.

But his immediate reaction worried me.

A gross overreaction to something that I wasn't sure Arnold could even enforce. And if Chase went through with it, one day, he'd blame me. Just like he'd thought that I would blame him if I didn't take the time to decide if I wanted to go to Harvard. But I'd taken that time, and now he needed it as well.

I shook my head. "That's not okay with me. You know what? I'm going to go stay with Bailey tonight."

"What?" he asked.

"Just take the time to think about it, Chase. We went longer in the past."

Then, I grabbed my purse off of the table and walked out the door. My heart constricted painfully as I got into my Kia and pulled away. Had I made the right choice?

All I'd wanted for the last three years was Chase Sinclair, and now, I was putting that all on the line. But I wouldn't be the reason he ruined his life, and he didn't seem to see what the problem was.

16

HARLEY

"Look what the cat dragged in," Bailey said when I appeared at Whitt's house later that night.

Bailey had been staying with Whitt and Eve since our housing situation had gone up in flames at the start of the summer. She was moving into a new apartment with friends from her program when the term resumed. But right now, that meant I was at my brother's for the evening.

"Hilarious."

"First, you kick me out of our house," she said as she tossed the door open wide. "Now, you come crawling back to stay with me. I don't know if I can survive this push and pull, Harley."

"I love you, Bails. You're fucking ridiculous."

"I love you, too. You going to tell me what happened?"

"Are Whitt and Eve here?"

Bailey shrugged. "They were out on a date. They should be back soon. I don't know. I'm not keeping up with them. It's weird to be back."

I could see that. Bailey had lived here her senior year of high school, but now, two years into her bachelors, she probably missed the independence.

"So, is this a *chick flick and ice cream* evening or a *plot murder* kind of evening?" she asked, heading toward the fridge.

I laughed. "How did you know?"

She shot me a look. "As if you'd show up here out of nowhere on a Saturday night. Weren't you having dinner with Chase's dad tonight?"

"Right." I winced. "That happened. Well, I guess dinner didn't happen."

"Right. Ice cream or murder?"

"Ice cream."

"Damn," she said as she reached into the freezer and pulled out pints of Blue Bell. "I was hoping for murder. Next time."

"There's no one to murder."

"Chase's dad, I'm assuming, would be a good option."

"He's a dick."

"Obviously. He preyed on my sister," Bailey said. Eve had been one of Arnold's earlier victims and he'd destroyed her life until she and Whitt had gotten together. "I despise him, and I can't imagine you being able to tolerate someone like that."

"No," I agreed with a sigh. "No, we really did not get along. But I think more because I'm a Wright. Though you should have seen him with his baby mama."

"Ew." Bailey shuddered. "That could have been Eve."

"Eve isn't that stupid. I think this girl wanted a kid."

"She trapped him?"

I shrugged, uncertain. Dayna had seemed nice and like she was doing the best with a bad situation. I couldn't imagine wanting to trap Arnold Sinclair.

"Just an accident, if I had to guess. Though Silas is adorable. So, I can't imagine she's upset with how it turned out, except for who the father is."

Bailey passed me a bowl of chocolate chip cookie dough and scooped out hers next.

"Yeah, can't get much slimier. So, what did he say to upset you?"

"He said I was like Owen."

Bailey waved her spoon at me. "Not Arnold. Chase."

I bit my lip. "Why do you think Chase did something to upset me?"

She shot me a disbelieving look. "Because I know you."

I took a bite of the ice cream and said nothing. How did I even begin to explain what the fuck had just happened? I'd been furious at Arnold, yes. He was despicable in every sense of the word. But I'd also expected him to upset me. I'd sort of prepared myself for his villainy. Owen had prepared me, to be honest. The way he'd treated Dayna set me on fucking fire, but was it anything worse than I'd expected? No.

But then Chase had gone and quit his job.

I stuffed more ice cream in my mouth. Fuck.

"That bad?" Bailey asked.

We flopped down onto the couch, and she flipped on *Romancing the Stone*. She was a sucker for '80s romances, especially those with Jack Colton–esque characters. Like the time that Chase dressed up as Indiana Jones. My heart ached at the thought. I shouldn't be thinking about him right now. It only made it all worse.

"I don't know," I said softly.

"You?" she asked, gobsmacked. "You don't know? Come on. You're, like, the smartest person I know. You know what he did. Spit it out."

"It's going to sound dumb."

"If it was dumb, you wouldn't be here."

I sighed and spilled the details of what had happened with Chase after we got back. Bailey scoffed at first, but then as more and more of the uncomfortable truths spewed out of me, her disbelief diminished.

"Damn," she muttered. "Well, at first, I thought, who cared that he quit? Fuck him. But I see your point of view."

"It's not stupid?"

"That you broke up with him because he'd quit his job over you?"

I nearly jumped out of my seat. "We didn't break up!"

Bailey reared back with wide eyes. "Whoa there, smartypants! Take a seat. It sure sounded like a breakup."

I shook my head. "No. I mean, I don't think so. Oh my God, does he think we broke up?"

"Uh, I don't know. Maybe you're on a break."

My heart raced ahead at that thought. "We're not on a break! Stop saying that!"

She held her hands up. "Okay, okay. Breathe. I didn't mean to freak you out. I don't have words for walking out of your boyfriend's house because you're mad at him and telling him to fucking figure it out. What happens if he doesn't figure it out, Harley Davidson?"

My stomach bottomed out at those words. I didn't want to even think about that. I'd walked out, knowing that he needed time to reconsider his stupid decision. He couldn't quit his job because his dad had said something mean about me. Like, that would never work in the long run.

I hadn't meant we were breaking up. He'd done the same thing to me when I was debating about Harvard. And, yeah, I'd originally decided to go and leave him behind. He could make that decision, too. Would we break up then?

I wanted to vomit at that thought. Three years we'd been apart. Three years where I'd wanted him more and more each day that passed. It should have been easy to just say, *Whatever. I don't care about your decision.* I could have stayed and pretended like it didn't matter.

But it *did* matter.

All of it fucking mattered. He couldn't give up on his dreams to be with me. That wasn't ever going to fly for me. I'd chosen a different path that included him. A path I'd chosen not because of him, but for myself. He was going to have to do the same. He wasn't stupid enough to not see the light.

"That's not going to happen," I told Bailey.

"Okay. I hope you're right."

"I want him to choose me," I blurted out.

Bailey polished off her ice cream and then tucked her legs underneath her. "Hasn't he already chosen you?"

"Yes, but this is different. He can quit. If that's what he wants, he can quit, obviously. I don't think he wants that.

And I don't want to be the scapegoat he uses later if he decides he fucked up."

"That's fair."

"But what if he doesn't come to that conclusion? I don't know. What if he thinks it's stupid?"

"That doesn't sound like him, but if it does happen, then you have to decide what you're going to do."

My panicked expression must have been answer enough.

Bailey put her hand on mine. "What do you want to happen?"

"I want him," I whispered. I set my ice cream down and came to my feet. "You don't understand. Chase Sinclair is all I have wanted for the last three years. Now that I have him, the very last thing I ever want is for it to end. I want it to be forever and ever, amen."

"Right. I was there, remember?"

"For some of it," I said. "But I love him. I love him so fucking much that it hurts. I can't imagine breaking up." I choked on the words. "I can't even say them. Oh my God. I can't even think them. It feels like my insides are on fire at the mere mention. And at the same time, I can't do nothing. Not when we spent three years apart so that we could make the right decision. Fuck, it doesn't even make sense."

"You're just in limbo, and you hate it."

"Yes," I said on a sigh. "I hate the anxiety of not knowing what he's thinking. But I don't want to go to him. He has to come to me. He has to make the decision on his own. And then we can figure it out together."

"That sounds like a decision."

"Does it?" I asked helplessly. "It sounds like doing nothing."

"Sometimes, doing nothing is the right option. You told him what you wanted and needed from him. You put the ball in his court. You can't fix anything before he decides what he's going to do."

"I know."

"But you hate it."

"Waiting and not knowing? Yes, I hate it." I shook my hands out. "I want him to just have never said that to his father."

"What's done is done. You can't go back, only forward."

"I know." I sighed, sinking back into my seat. "So, sit and wait to hear from him?"

She grasped my hand. "He's going to come to the right conclusion. He's not *that* dumb."

I laughed humorlessly. "Yeah. Yeah, you're right."

But it didn't make me feel any better. I'd made the right choice, and it felt worse than ever. Being away from him felt like death. I wished that I could erase the entire night and get a do-over, but I couldn't. And until I heard from Chase, I just had to sit in my discomfort.

17

CHASE

I parked my Subaru outside of Annie's house. She hadn't answered any of my texts, which only happened when she was on shift at the hospital, but she'd told me earlier this week that she had the weekend off. Maybe she'd been called in anyway.

I could have called Kai.

I should have called Kai.

But part of me knew that only Annie could help me through the nightmare that was my current situation. The fucking hell I'd walked headfirst into.

With my hands stuffed into my jeans, I lurched toward the door and pressed the doorbell. It rang noisily into the confines of that giant Wright house. I'd only been here once or twice. Usually, if I saw Annie anymore, it was at my place because of the Wright problem within. But today was necessary.

The door slid open, and Jordan Wright stood before me with an arched eyebrow. He was in a button-up and slacks, as if he was about to throw on his jacket and head out to the office. But it was a Saturday in the middle of the summer. Where the hell would he be going?

"Hey," I muttered.

"No solicitors," he said and then moved to shut the door in my face.

I slapped my hand down on the door. "I just need to talk to Annie."

Jordan sighed. "Must you?"

"It's important."

He released his grip on the door, and I pushed it all the way open, following him inside when he retreated into the depths.

"Annie, you have an unwanted visitor," he yelled into the house.

"Thanks, Jordan."

"Don't thank me yet."

I just shook my head at him. There was no point really. He was always going to be this way. In some ways, it was reassuring. Things would change; Jordan's dislike of me would always stay the same.

Annie stepped out of the bedroom in scrubs. Her hair was mussed, and her eyes were bloodshot. She yawned. "What's going on?" Her eyes snagged on me. "Oh, Chase, what are you doing here?"

"Did you just come off a shift?"

"Yeah. I got called in and spent the last twelve hours working an extra shift. I was about to shower and crawl into bed for some much needed TLC."

"Whiskey instead?" I offered.

She narrowed her eyes. "What's going on?"

"Need to talk to you. I tried to text, and you didn't answer."

Her eyes flicked to Jordan, who still hadn't moved from where he stood in the living room.

He raised his hands. "I don't have anything to do with this."

"Can I shower first?" she asked.

"By all means. I'll just hang out with your husband."

She frowned and then pointed at Jordan. "Don't kill each other."

"You're no fun," he teased.

Annie pointed stronger. "Jordan Wright."

He winked at her, and she just rolled her eyes, disappearing into their bedroom. A minute later, I could hear the water running in the bathroom.

Jordan turned to me then. "You said whiskey?"

I was wary but nodded. "That kind of night."

Jordan headed to the liquor cabinet. "I'd ask if you have a preference," he said, pulling out a bottle of Basil Hayden, "but I really don't care."

"Basil Hayden is fine," I said.

"Pity."

He passed me a glass of the whiskey and poured himself one as well. This was as close as Jordan and I had ever been to civil. Almost, dare I say it, friendly.

"Don't stay too long," Jordan said as he strode back across the room. "I had other plans for Annie tonight."

Okay. Maybe friendly was too far.

"Noted," I muttered, giving him a two-finger salute as he disappeared.

Fifteen minutes later, my drink was empty, and Annie

had returned from her shower. Her red curls were wet and hanging past her shoulders. She'd replaced her scrubs with cotton shorts and a tank top. After I poured myself another drink, she grabbed the bottle out of my hand and set it back in its place.

"What's up? You never come here," she said.

"No, but I figured I should talk to you."

"About?"

I glanced back to make sure Jordan was still out of earshot. "Harley."

She sighed and sank into a seat at the bar. "What happened?"

"Harley and I were going to have dinner with my dad."

Her green eyes rounded to the size of saucers. "Why the fuck would you do *that*?"

"I wanted for him to meet her."

"Did he *want* to meet her?"

"Well, he didn't know who I was dating."

Annie's mouth popped open. "You ambushed your father with your Wright girlfriend?"

"It wasn't an ambush," I grumbled.

She held her hand up. "Wait, wait, wait, what did you think your dad was going to do when you showed up with a Wright? Because I can tell you what I think probably happened."

"What do you think happened?"

"That he blew a gasket, Chase. Of course he did. He was humiliated by Wrights at a public event and lost the favor of the *mayor*. He doesn't even work with us anymore because of all of it. He *hates* us."

"Us," he muttered.

She shrugged. "Hate to break it to you, but I'm a Wright, too."

"I know," he said. "Jordan wouldn't let me forget."

"Anyway, did he blow up?"

"Yeah."

"Is Harley okay? I'm sure he wasn't kind."

I frowned and downed the rest of the whiskey. "She's upset with me."

"To put it mildly?"

"She walked out."

Annie sighed heavily. Then, she reached back for the bottle of whiskey and refilled my glass. "You probably need that. I can't imagine it's easy to see her hurting."

Jordan cleared his throat behind us. I jumped. I hadn't been paying attention to him. I'd figured he'd left us alone. Fuck.

"Did you say Harley is hurting?"

"Jordan," Annie warned.

"That's not what happened," I told him.

"You do remember me telling you that I'd kill you if you hurt her, right?"

"Jordan!" Annie cried.

Jordan shrugged. "Bold of you to come to my house after hurting my sister."

"She's the one who walked out," I said, holding my hands up.

Jordan laughed. "Well, that's the smartest thing she's done in a while."

"Ha-ha," I said with an eye roll. "Just what I needed—to be kicked when I'm down."

"I can try harder," he offered.

"Ignore him," Annie said. "Why did she leave anyway? What did your dad say?"

"He compared her to Owen."

Jordan flinched. "Ah. Yeah, she's not going to be happy about that."

"She wasn't, but then my dad and I got into it. And he said I couldn't work at the company while dating a Wright. So, I quit."

Annie and Jordan both stared at me in stunned silence. I drained the rest of my glass. Yeah, that was what I'd thought, too. That I'd done the right thing. I wasn't going to give in to his bullshit. And yet Harley had acted like I was destroying our relationship by making that decision.

"You can't quit," Annie said.

"That's not enforceable," Jordan said at the same time.

They glanced at each other and laughed.

"Look at Jordan defending you," Annie muttered.

"I wasn't defending him," Jordan said, sliding his arm around her middle. "But I grew up with Owen. I know these sorts of games. He can't fire you. Not while you're the public face of the company. The board would have to do it. If you quit, you're giving him what he wants."

"No, what he wants is me and Harley not together."

"And you're currently not," Annie pointed out.

I jerked back at those words. Fuck. Fuck, fuck, fuck. Were we broken up? No, it hadn't been like that. She wanted to give me some space. Fuck, was it space? I didn't want space. Not like that. No, she wanted me to figure this out. I'd given her all the space that she needed to make her decision about Harvard. If I was going to make one about the company, then I should probably make it with more thought than rising to my father's bait.

Fuck, was she right?

"I don't want to encourage you to right things with my sister," Jordan said. "She can do better."

"Thanks," I grumbled.

"But she's fucking smart, and Owen trained her up well. She probably saw that you were getting played before you did. If she's miffed about this shit, then you should probably listen to her."

"He's right," Annie said. She smiled up at her husband, clearly pleased that she'd gotten him on board. "Basically, you're being a fucking idiot."

"So glad that's the general consensus."

"Just think for a second. Do you still want to work for the company? Can you still work with your father? Do you think things will change once you all calm down?"

"That's what Harley wanted me to think about."

Annie nodded. "And she's right."

"She thinks I'll resent her if I quit because of the bull-shit with my dad."

"Wouldn't you?"

I opened my mouth to deny it. I never could resent or regret her. Not a second. But instead, I let the anger go, and I really thought about it. I loved my job. My father aside, the job was great. It was what I'd always wanted. If I quit because I was with Harley, would I put that back on her? I wanted to say no, but I didn't know. Hadn't we spent all of that time apart just so that she could be sure? Didn't I owe it to her to be sure here too?

"Fuck."

Annie patted my arm. "Figured it out?"

"I fucked up."

Jordan shook his head. "You can say that again."

"What am I going to do?"

"Figure the stuff out with work before you go back to her. I bet she needs the time to collect herself anyway," Annie said with a sad smile. "I've been on the other end of this *idiot doing stupid shit without talking to me*. You need to get it together."

"Hey!" Jordan said.

"Yeah," I said, putting my head in my hands. "Fucking fuck."

"Just have another drink. Figure it out in the morning."

She poured more whiskey into my cup.

"If I drink much more, I won't be able to drive."

"Crash in the guest room," she told me.

My eyes lifted to Jordan. I certainly never would have thought that Jordan Wright would welcome me into his home. Not like that.

But he just nodded. "Not going to endanger my sister's boyfriend."

Annie snorted. "Right."

"Well, not any more than I already have."

"Thanks," I said and meant it.

"Fuck off," he said with a smile.

I laughed as Jordan pulled Annie into the kitchen to grab her some dinner. She apparently hadn't had a break to eat at the hospital. Watching them together made me realize just how much I wanted this with Harley. And how stupid I'd been to jump to conclusions and let my father bait me.

I'd fix this.

I'd fucking fix this.

18

HARLEY

Waiting was torture.

Whitt and Eve were happy to see me lounging on their couch when they came home from their date. It immediately shifted to concern when it was clear it was not a leisurely visit. Keeping Whitt from hunting Chase down was an effort in civility. Eve and Bailey pitched in.

Especially because Chase hadn't really hurt me. Not the way Whitt was thinking. But we were still on the rocks. Which made my stomach hurt.

I went to bed, restless and feeling sick, and woke up feeling worse. I could just text or call him and see where his head was at, but I also *couldn't* do that. He needed the time.

I had a new appreciation for how hard it must have been for Chase to wait and see with me. Knowing that he'd wanted me the whole time and that he also needed to give me space. He'd been right then, and I was right now.

Bailey cooked me a fancy breakfast, and we watched more '80s rom-coms. It was a pleasant distraction while my stomach was rumbling uncertainly. I didn't know how long I'd have to stay here. Luckily, I could fit into Bailey's clothes even though she was taller than me, but I wouldn't be able to do that for work on Monday. I'd have to find time to go home and get clothes. Should I send Bailey on a reconnaissance mission for me?

Ugh!

The idea of being here another whole day, let alone having to sneak back into my house to get clothes to go to work, was depressing. I was going to break before then. I could feel it. Even though Bailey insisted that I wouldn't. I'd never done it before. But this was Chase.

Bailey popped into the shower while I was doom-scrolling on my phone after lunch when the text came through.

Meet me at the lake? Our spot?

My heart leaped. Chase.

Radio silence for nearly twenty-four hours, and now, he wanted me to meet him at the lake? That was pretty ballsy of him. I didn't even have a change of clothes. I wasn't going to just pretend nothing had happened. Even if I'd thought about it all night.

For what?

To talk.

Why can't we talk at home?

Harley, please, our spot. I'll meet you there.

I wanted to shoot back that I didn't have a change of clothes. That I didn't want to drive twenty minutes out of Lubbock to have this conversation. I wanted to know where his head was at *right now*. But that was just my own impatience.

I'd meet him.

Of course I'd fucking meet him.

I rapped on the bathroom door in Bailey's room. She opened it, wrapped in a towel. "What's up?"

"Heard from Chase. I'm going to go meet him to talk."

She broke into a smile. "Good! I knew he'd come around. What did he say?"

"Nothing really, just that we should meet at the lake to talk."

Her brow furrowed. "Why the lake?"

"I don't know. It's our spot. I asked if we could talk at home, but he insisted."

"Well, this is good, right?" Bailey sounded hopeful. "I'm sure this is good."

"Can I borrow a change of clothes?" I gestured to her grungy sweats I was wearing.

"Raid my closet. I'm sure there's something black in there."

I rolled my eyes at her, but did just that. In fact, I found one of my *own* dresses in there. I held the ruffled-sleeve black dress up and arched an eyebrow at her. "Stealing my shit?"

Bailey laughed. "It's too long on you!"

"No, it isn't! You thief," I said with a laugh.

Suddenly, everything felt lighter at the prospect of seeing Chase. I didn't even know what he was going to say, but at least we were going to figure it out. I couldn't sit around another day and wait. How had he gone months, waiting for me?

I threw the dress over my head. Despite Bailey's insistence, the dress fit perfect. Maybe better than the last time I'd remembered wearing it. My finger went to the *H* pendant necklace around my neck. I'd considered taking it off last night, but I'd just tucked it into my shirt. Now, I pulled it back out, on display.

Then I hugged Bailey, thanked her for the girl time, and then headed out of the house to see my man.

***

The dirt road to our spot at Buffalo Springs Lake was dry and dusty. We were in a drought, as per usual in the summer, but it seemed even dustier than normal. Chase's Subaru was parked in the dirt nearby. He'd laid out a blanket on the shoreline. No Bowie in sight.

My heart beat furiously at the sight of him staring off at the water. His hands in the pockets of his khakis. A white Polo completing what was a dressed-down look for him. At least he'd kicked off his boat shoes and was standing barefoot, his eyes hidden behind Ray-Bans.

When he heard the engine coming down the hill, a smile graced his features. I parked next to his car and hopped out of the driver's side. It took real effort not to rush to him, throwing my arms around him and forgiving everything. It was all I wanted to do after all. But I needed to hear him out. Bailey's words ran continuously through my mind. What would happen if this didn't go how I wanted?

I swallowed and approached him, the wind whipping my blonde hair around my face. "Hey."

"Hey," he said.

"Did we have to drive all the way out here for this?"

"It's a nice day. No reason to spend it inside."

I furrowed my brow. It was nearly a hundred degrees at the end of July and boiling hot. The only way this would be enjoyable was if we stripped down and jumped in the lake. "It's a Texas summer."

"Assuredly."

"Chase, what am I doing here?"

I was starting to get nervous. He wasn't *saying* anything. Had I driven all the way out here for nothing?

"I had a rough night," he said.

"I bet. Mine wasn't exactly great either."

"I talked to Annie and Jordan."

"You talked to Jordan?" I gasped. I took a step toward him, inspecting his face. "You don't look damaged."

He grinned. "No, he promised to kill me, but thinks that you walking out was smart."

I snorted. "That sounds like him."

"Anyway, it's not about them. Though they think you were right to do what you did."

"I was...am," I said even though it felt terrible.

"I know you are."

I froze at those words. "You know I'm right?"

"Of course. I should have known right away."

"Then, why did it take you so long to talk to me?"

He brushed a hand back through his messy blond hair. "I didn't want to fuck this up. And I couldn't get you back without making sure that I did the right thing."

"Which was?"

"I called a few people on the board of the company. I wanted to make sure that they were aware of what had happened with my father." He sighed heavily. "Apparently, my father had already reached out and told them that I quit. He'd insisted that he was going to take back over my duties. They were planning to meet next week to discuss what to do with me out of the position."

"Oh fuck," I whispered.

"But I informed them that wasn't my intention. You were right. I don't want to leave. They know I'm doing more than my father is at this point. And his reaction to who I'm dating just makes him look unstable."

"They said that?" I asked hopefully. "I mean, he *is* unstable."

"He is. I don't know what decision they're going to make, but they said they would be in touch on Monday after they convened. In the meantime, my job is secure."

"That's a relief."

"And I'm sorry," he said, taking a step toward me and reaching for my hand. "I'm so fucking sorry. I was not in my right mind when I spoke with my dad, and then I took that out on you. Watching you walk out that door was a kick in the face. I hated it, but I needed it to remember what I really wanted."

A tear came to my eye, and I choked it back. "Well, I'm glad you came to your senses."

"Harley, I waited three years for you, and I would have waited the three years you were at Harvard. I would wait forever for you. Do you understand? The very last thing I want in this world is to be without you. Can you forgive me for disregarding your feelings?"

His eyes were so fucking earnest. His heart on his sleeve. I wanted to lean into that. I wanted to give in with every fiber of my being. I loved his apology, but I didn't just want an apology. I wanted to make sure it didn't happen again.

"What happens if this happens again?" I asked slowly.

"I can't promise that I'll always be levelheaded." He laughed softly. "Unfortunately, I was raised by my father. Just like you were raised by Owen. They both have their claws in us more than either of us could ever know. I hate when I find how deep those hooks go. I hate every time I'm more like him." His hand went to my cheek and tipped my face up to look at him. "But I can promise we can work it out together. That things might not be perfect, but as long as it's you and me, we can work it out."

I nodded. "Good. I want that."

"You do?"

"Of course I do!" I said with a quivery laugh. "I hate how much I'm like Owen, too. I hate that I can twist any argument around and how much I have to *win*. I've been trying to rein it in, but it's not easy to restructure who I am as a person. Maybe it's best that we both accept that some parts of our personalities are going to be works in progress. We can hold each other accountable."

"Anything for you. I want us to be a team."

"I want that, too," I said with a sniffle. "Now, kiss me, you dummy. I missed you so fucking much."

He laughed, both dimples appearing in full, and drew me into him. His lips slanted against mine, light and tempting. I wanted to devour him, but my body was still too shaky. I'd had all this anticipatory anxiety over the fact that we might have walked into a scenario both of us were too stubborn to walk out of. Instead, we'd come out stronger on the other side.

"I missed you, too," he said against my lips. "I love you."

"I love you," I said, pressing myself against him.

"But calling the board wasn't the only reason that you had to wait."

I pulled back just enough to arch an incredulous eyebrow. "What does that mean?"

Then, Chase put his hand back in his pocket and pulled out a small black box.

My brain couldn't process what I was seeing. That he was sliding from my grasp and to one knee. That his smile was magnetic as he looked up at me. That he popped the top of the box.

That there was a ring inside of it.

Then, I caught up. I gasped, my hand going to my mouth in disbelief.

This wasn't just *some* ring.

This was *the* ring.

My ring. I didn't even know how he could have found

something more *me* in the entire world. Who knew Lubbock, Texas, would even have something so unique and quintessentially me?

The center stone was a large black oval diamond, surrounded in a halo of smaller diamonds, on a gold band. It was delicate and badass, and if I'd ever wanted a wedding ring, this would have been the one.

"I spent the last twenty-four hours realizing that I never wanted to go a single day without you again. Not a single solitary day if I could help it. We had three years to make sure this was right, and I know it down to my bones that you're it. You're the one I love—mind, body, and soul. I can't promise perfection. Only that I will always be here to work on it with you, that I will always cherish your brilliant opinion, and I will always love you.

"Harley, will you marry me?"

"Oh my God," I whispered in disbelief. "Yes! Yes, yes, yes."

He laughed, coming to his feet and plucking the dainty band out of its box. He slid it onto my left hand, and I stared at it in awe before he wrapped his arms around my waist and swung me in a circle.

Twenty-four hours earlier, I'd been worried that this would be the end of us. And now, here I was, with a ring on my finger, knowing it was completely right.

"I don't want to wait," he said as he put me on my feet. "We've waited long enough."

I laughed. "What? Do you want to fly out to Vegas? My family will flip."

"I wasn't thinking Vegas." He smirked like he'd actually already planned this. "I was thinking...New Mexico."

"Are you serious?"

"There's a ski resort that's empty for the offseason," he said. "I happen to know the owner."

"Have you already spoken to Blake? Before you knew if I'd say yes?"

He shook his head. "No, but I know he'll say yes. What do you say? Elope with me? We'll deal with our families later. I've had enough of waiting for them to accept what we have. I want this to be for us. If you want, we can have a huge party when we get back."

"You're serious?"

"Dead serious."

My mind was firing on all cylinders, but I couldn't see a negative to this. I'd never been the kind of girl who dreamed of her big wedding day. When I thought of it now, the only thing I wanted was my groom there.

"Let's do it."

PART IV

——————

FOREVER

19

HARLEY

"Well, that makes sense."

I grinned at Bailey, thrusting my hand out to her. "Doesn't it?"

"This morning you thought you'd break up, and now, you're engaged."

"Yeah, fucking wild."

"Are you going to tell your brothers? Because I'm just imagining Whitt's face right now, and I would really like to see that."

I bit my lip. "That's actually why I asked you to meet. We're, um...eloping."

Bailey tipped her head up. "Like, to Vegas?"

"New Mexico actually."

Bailey opened her mouth and then closed it.

"We're going to Holliday Ski."

"Oh," she said.

"Blake is going to meet us. I want you two to be our witnesses."

"Me...and Blake?" she repeated.

"Yes! I know you two hooked up, so there's tension, but…"

"There isn't tension," she said, her voice flat.

"Uh-huh."

"It was a one-night stand. I left my number. He never called. It's whatever."

I shot her a disbelieving look. "Okay. If you're still upset about it, then you don't have to go."

"One," she said, holding up a finger, "I'm not upset about it. He was a good lay—a great lay, mind you—but he's just a guy."

"Yet you left your number," I said under my breath.

"Regardless. And two, I am not fucking missing you eloping in the New Mexico mountains! Are you insane?"

I laughed. "Good. I really want you to be there."

"But no one else? Are you sure?"

"I'm sure. We've spent *so* long worrying more about what our families would think than about what we wanted. I know things were rocky before. I thought that I might freak out, but the more I think about it, the more excited I am. This is what I want."

"Without your family?"

I nudged her in the arm. "We can have another ceremony or reception here after. We want this to just be us. I don't want to have to deal with the drama. I love him. We want to get married. We're doing it."

"Okay," she said with a shrug. "Well, I'm here for new, impulsive Harley. Let's get you hitched."

"Which is another reason I called you." I bit my lip uncertainly. "I need a dress."

"Ohhh," Bailey said. "Oh my God, you want me to go wedding dress shopping with you?"

"Would you?"

"I was made for this. You have to try on every single one in the store."

"I will try on everything that is in my size because we don't have time to get it altered...since we're leaving today."

Bailey sputtered, "Today!"

"Yeah. If you're free..."

"Fuck yes! Let's do it!"

After an hour of trying on so many dresses that I'd lost count, I finally walked out of the store with the perfect dress. I held it against my chest reverently as we walked back to the car.

"Chase is going to die," Bailey said.

"I can't believe this was *on sale*, too," I said, hugging the bag tighter. "What a steal."

"It was meant to be." Bailey held up her own dress. "And something for me, too."

"Yes, my maid of honor."

Bailey's wide smile was the best result. We piled our dresses into the cars and promised to meet at Chase's within the hour, ready to leave for the mountains. I kept glancing back at the dress in the rearview mirror as I drove back to the house.

I carried it inside like it was made out of glass, and Chase stalled at the sight of it.

"Is that what I think it is?"

"Yes, and you can't see it until tomorrow."

"You found what you were looking for?"

"You'll have to wait and see," I teased. "I need to pack."

"Can I get a sneak peek?"

He reached for the dress, and I jerked it away from him.

"Absolutely not."

He laughed. "Fair. I won't peek. I want my first look to be you walking down the aisle to me."

I melted at that, leaning in for a kiss. "You better be packed and ready. Bailey agreed to come with. Have you definitely heard from Blake?"

"I did. He got his sister, Ivy, working on it. He said not to worry about a thing, that they'd have it handled."

"Okay. I guess I am not worrying about a thing, except packing."

He pressed a kiss to my lips, pulling me in close. "If you're quick, we can have a quickie before we go."

"Oh no," I said. I slid out of his arms. "Don't you know you're not supposed to have sex before the wedding?"

He blinked at me. "We've been having sex for three years."

"Well then, you can wait one night," I teased.

"You're trying to torture me."

"Nope! I want you to want me so badly that we have wild wedding night sex."

He chuckled. "And you think we won't have that if you don't abstain?"

"Fair," I said with a shrug as I backed into the bedroom. "Guess we won't find out."

I heard his frustrated groan as I shut the door in his face. It was probably a stupid tradition, but we were doing literally everything else on our own terms. I wanted this one thing. Not because it was necessary or anything to do with virginity, which obviously had nothing to do with this situation. But just so it would be special. And he couldn't change my mind.

Well, maybe he could. He was pretty persuasive with his tongue.

I shut down that line of thought and hurried to my closet to pack.

The drive into New Mexico was about four hours from Lubbock. Long enough that we were all tired and ready to crash by the time we got there. But not too long for most Texas drives. When everything was a four- or five-hour drive, you got used to it.

Blake met us at the entrance after we parked in the mostly empty parking lot. He was in a black suit and had a radiant smile on his stupid-pretty face. His dark hair was brushed back, and his big brown eyes were glittering with excitement.

Then, his gaze slid from me and Chase to Bailey, and he faltered. The smile stilling for a second as he realized who we'd brought with us. When I'd first met Blake, I'd assumed he wasn't the kind of guy who could get side-lined by the appearance of a girl. Chase had always made him seem like the consummate playboy bachelor. And yet the way he was looking at Bailey right now showed that wasn't entirely true. She threw him off-balance, and I liked it.

"Hey, Blake," Chase said, holding his hand out to his friend.

He ripped his gaze from Bailey and clapped his hand into his friend's. "Chase, so glad that you're here. And with your beautiful fiancée."

Fiancée.

My heart stuttered at that word. I hadn't even thought the word despite the rock currently on my finger. It was all so surreal.

He let Chase go to shake my hand. "Can't believe this guy is getting hitched, but it had to be you, of course."

"It did," Chase said. "There was never anyone else."

"Bailey," he said, offering her his hand.

She had an amused look on her face. Then, she took another step into him and put her hand in his. "Hi, Blake."

"Good to have you back at Holliday Ski."

"Perfect time of year for me actually."

"No skiing?" he guessed.

"Hot tub still works, I hear."

"Year-round," he said, still holding her hand in his.

"Excellent."

Chase cleared his throat. "Shall we check in?"

"Yes, yes," he said, dropping Bailey's hand. "Let me introduce you to Ivy. Chase knows her, but for the rest of you. She's in charge of basically everything. She's going to make the day perfect."

We strode inside, and I was shocked to see the place was *empty*. Of course, I'd known it would be empty, but it was different seeing it bare. I'd only ever been here in season. I hadn't imagined what it would look like in the middle of the summer when no one was here. It was almost sad to see the huge, beautiful space not crowded with people. The snow dictated their entire lives.

A leggy brunette was standing at the reception desk when we approached. She tucked an iPad under her arm and shook our hands. "Good to see you, Chase. This must be Harley."

"That's me," I told her.

"Excellent. I'm Ivy Holliday."

"Nice to meet you."

"It's so good to have you at Holliday Ski. We had rooms prepared ahead of time. I wasn't sure if you wanted separate rooms and then move into the honeymoon suite after the wedding or if you wanted to stay in there now. We let our couples choose." She passed a key to Bailey.

"Suite is fine," Chase said at the same time I said, "Separate."

He laughed. "We're on this again."

"Just for tonight."

Ivy nodded. "Of course."

She handed out separate keys to us while Chase looked ready to argue. But Ivy seemed to be no-nonsense, and already, she was walking us around the property.

We could do nothing but follow her.

We saw the ceremony space, the spa and fitness

center, as well as the bar, and salon, and the empty five-star restaurant on-site. Our luggage was already in our rooms, and if we needed anything, we were told to act like we owned the place. Because, ostensibly, for the weekend, we did.

"Hey, Bailey," Blake said as we headed toward the elevators for our rooms.

I paused to wait for her, but she waved me off.

"I'm a big girl," she said. "Have fun with your fiancé."

"You're sure?"

"Course," she said and headed for Blake.

Oh, those two were trouble.

Chase and I took the elevator to the top floor.

He tapped the key card against his palm a few times before saying, "We could still take the honeymoon suite."

"I'm not budging on this one."

He slipped his arms around me and stole a kiss. "I thought we were doing this so we didn't have to spend time away from each other."

I laughed. "It's *one* night."

"I spent last night away from you, too."

"Two nights won't kill us. We went months and *years* in the past, Chase. By this time tomorrow, I'll be all yours."

"You already are," he said. "This time tomorrow, you'll be my wife."

I shivered at those words, feeling indulgent with desire at them. Yeah, if he kept talking like that, I was going to give in and stay in his room.

"I can't wait to be your wife," I told him. The elevator

dinged, and I stepped backward out of it. "But you can have me all you want tomorrow."

"Devious," he said as he followed me.

"Tomorrow," I promised. "However you want me."

"However?"

I nodded, tugging him in for one more kiss. "That's a promise."

Then, I opened the door to my room in the lodge and closed the door behind me. I leaned back against it, unable to believe that we were here, doing this.

Tomorrow, Chase Sinclair would be my husband.

20

CHASE

Blake handed me a drink.

I gulped and then took it from him. "Thanks."

"Can't believe you're eloping, dude."

I shrugged and took a sip of whiskey. He wasn't wrong. This was not my normal behavior, but it was Harley, and so it felt perfectly right.

"I mean, you're sort of the definition of follow the rules. But not with Harley." He punched me on the arm. "I like that she brings that out in you."

"Me too."

"And this is what you want?" he asked as he tossed back his drink.

"Yes," I said forcefully.

"Good." He nodded his head at me and leaned back against the bar.

The girls had been at the spa and salon all morning, doing who knew what. Ashleigh would have known, but I didn't have any interest in my meddlesome sister being here. In fact, I was glad that it was just us. That was what

I wanted. No second-guessing, no drama, no wondering if Wrights and Sinclairs were going to come to blows as she walked down the aisle. All that mattered was that this was what we wanted. The rest could be worked out later.

Maybe Blake was right that this wasn't me. I wouldn't have ever even thought about something like this before Harley. I'd dated Kennedy for years before I even let her move in let alone before I bought a ring. Annie and I'd had a marriage pact for a decade. None of those situations had been right.

Meanwhile, Harley had moved in basically as soon as we started dating, and only a few months later, I was so certain I wanted to marry her that I'd engineered an elopement. Fuck everything else in my life. Harley was the one constant that I knew for certain was right.

"What about you?" I asked Blake.

"Me? You know, same old, same old."

I shot him a look. "And Bailey?"

He cocked an eyebrow. "What about her?"

"All right. If that's how you want to play it. I'll pretend I didn't see you miss a whole fucking step at the sight of her."

"She's...not like other girls," he admitted.

I laughed. "Oh fucking hell, man. You're screwed, aren't you?"

"Screwed up, you mean," he said. "I definitely screwed it up."

"What do you mean?"

"Nothing. Never mind."

"You can't leave me hanging like that."

Blake blew out a breath. "All right. Last time, we hooked up, and she left her number, but I never called."

"As per usual."

"Right. Right." He gestured to me. "I treated her just like any other girl."

"Oh, I see where this is going."

"Yeah. She didn't like that."

"I don't think any of the girls like it, man."

Blake poured himself more whiskey. "It's never mattered before. I thought it wouldn't matter with her either. When I saw her yesterday, I thought we'd have a fun weekend."

I smirked and waited for him to finish that thought. Bailey had stayed out with him last night. Surely, they'd had the night he had imagined. No one turned Blake Holliday down.

"So, what happened?" I prompted when he was still lost in thought.

"She turned me down!" he said in frustration. "We had a drink. We were talking up late. And when I made my move, she walked."

I could barely contain the laughter bubbling up in me. "Maybe you should have called."

"Maybe I should have," he said thoughtfully. "Now, she won't give me the time of day."

"No more than you deserve."

His eyes were distant for a moment. "It's probably fine, right? She'll come around."

"Uh, you're probably going to have to earn her trust back."

He looked at me skeptically. Blake had never had to work for anything in his life. He'd been handed nearly everything on a silver spoon. Working for a girl's attention for her trust was not in his cards. He didn't even know what that meant.

But he wasn't getting anywhere with Bailey if he didn't try. Which made me think…he wasn't going to get anywhere with Bailey. I wished I'd gotten to see the look on his face when she turned him down.

"We'll see," Blake said. "But we're here for your wedding, man. Let's focus on what's important."

I laughed and let him change the topic. That was fine. He probably had a fight ahead of him, and he'd have to figure that out on his own.

Hours later, I stood at the center of the lodge with floor-to-ceiling windows that overlooked the bare ski slopes beyond. I faced a grand staircase that spilled out into the lodge from above. In the winter, a towering Christmas tree took up most of the space with twinkling lights on every available surface. But today, the room was lit by the summer sun. The smell of a dozen enormous bouquets littered the tables. I wasn't sure if Ivy had brought them in for the wedding or if they were always there. Either way, it brightened the room.

Part of me had wanted to wear a black suit for the occasion, but I couldn't help myself when I pulled my tuxedo out of the back of my closet. It felt right. So, I'd gone with it. Blake stood next to me in his. Though he'd grumbled when I made him get his out. He was the witness on my side.

The only other people in attendance were the rest of Blake's siblings—Caleb, Griffin, and Ivy—a pianist, Tawa, that they kept on staff, and the officiant, Hannah, who had shown up early to review the planned ceremony with me. She'd asked if we'd written our own vows, but on short notice, there hadn't been time. She promised that she had it all covered. Now, her hands were crossed in front of her, and she was watching the staircase in anticipation with the rest of us.

With a gesture from Ivy, Tawa shifted from the song he had been playing to another softer tune. I held my breath as Bailey appeared at the top of the staircase. She was in a knee-length black slip dress and held a small bouquet of white flowers. The salon had clearly known what they were doing because her dark hair was down past her shoulders in gentle waves, and her makeup was light with a dark pink lipstick. She smiled at me encouragingly before taking up her place on the bride's side.

Tawa changed to Canon in D, and something in my chest tightened. The bridal march made me straighten. Blake patted my back encouragingly. It was time.

Harley walked to the edge of the staircase, and I took her in, in all her splendor.

Her wedding dress was black.

Of course it was black. Of fucking course it was.

A laugh bubbled to the surface. I didn't know why I'd thought anything else. In my head, I'd assumed white. Even though I'd only seen her in white a handful of times when it wasn't also paired with black. But my little Halloween queen would have to be in black.

The bodice was a collection of black petals, hand-sewn to cover the corset top and then running down the full black tulle skirt. Little shimmery black beads and jewels were sewn around the petals to give it dimension. A black mesh came up to her neck, tying in a bow at the back, with matching billowy sleeves, sewn with more of the petal work. The sleeves were tight at her wrists, and I could see the black diamond I'd put on her left hand glittering in the light.

She held a large bouquet of white flowers to offset all the black and made her way down the stairs. With one perfect kick to keep the dress out from under her feet, I got a glimpse of her footwear. Doc Martens. She'd worn her Docs to the wedding. God, I fucking loved her.

Her bleached-blonde hair was down to her shoulders, but she'd had them chop her bangs into feathery wisps, framing her round face. Her makeup was natural, all except for the dark red of her lips that looked like she'd just dipped them in her favorite wine.

All in all, she was a stunning visage, and I couldn't believe she was mine.

She passed Bailey the flowers and finally stopped in front of me. "Hi," she whispered.

I took her hands in mine, pulling them to my lips and pressing a kiss to them. I couldn't resist. "Hi."

"Fancy meeting you here."

"Your dress is black."

She glanced down at it and then grinned back up at

me. "Pretty lucky find, huh? It's a winter dress, so it was even on sale."

I chuckled. "I love you."

"Convenient. I love you, too."

Hannah cleared her throat. "Why don't we begin?"

Harley faced the officiant, but my eyes were still only for my bride. My brilliant, fierce, loyal, incredible, stunning, opinionated bride. I couldn't believe we were doing it. I couldn't believe I hadn't thought of it sooner.

Hannah pulled out a small iPad and began to read, "We are gathered here today to join Chase and Harley in matrimony. After just a short time in their presence, I can tell that the love they share is a once-in-a-lifetime love and that this union is blessed from the start.

"Now, for the vows. Chase, repeat after me. *I promise to cherish you always...*"

"I promise to cherish you always," I spoke directly to Harley. "To honor and love you, in sickness and in health, rich or poor, and all the challenges that may come. I will always be true to you until death do us part."

Harley sniffled at the words and then repeated them back to me. My heart felt close to bursting when I heard them from her. Watching her big silvery-blue eyes fill with emotion as she told me how she was mine forever.

"You have the rings," Hannah said.

"Rings," Harley said, frantic for a moment.

But I'd handled this, too.

Blake reached into the pocket of his tux and pulled the bands out. Harley hadn't seen what I'd picked for her. My ring was a standard silver band that I was going to have engraved with our wedding date when we got home. I passed the ring to her.

"A ring is a symbol of your unending union. The unbroken circle that signifies eternity for your love. You are joined together today and from this day forth with infinite love. Cherish it always as a symbol of how you feel about each other."

Harley took my hand in hers and held the ring before my finger. "With this ring, I take you, Chase Sinclair, to be my husband with a pledge of love today, tomorrow, and for always."

She slid the ring home with a choked gasp. Her eyes were still on mine, and I reached up and brushed a stray tear from her cheek.

"Now, Chase," Hannah said.

I retrieved the ring from Blake, and with all the emotion still in my voice, I held it out to her . Her eyes found the ring as I repeated the same words to her. Her jaw dropped open at the sight of the wedding ring which was pointed in an arrow of small black diamonds on a gold band that perfectly fit against the engagement ring.

"Chase," she whispered after I finished, "it's perfect."

"Just like you."

Hannah smiled at the pair of us. "These rings are a pledge before witnesses of your commitment to one another. By the power vested in me, I now pronounce you man and wife. You may kiss your bride."

I swept Harley into my arms, twisting and dipping her. She relaxed into my grip, our eyes locked. There was a little smirk on her lips, and I covered them with my own, claiming her as mine.

21

HARLEY

*B*ride.
Wife.
Mine.

Those were the words Chase had spoken to me. The words that we'd uttered to each other before a small audience as the sun began to sink toward the horizon. And now, we were married.

I stared down at the rings on my finger as we took the elevator up to the top floor. He knew me mind, body, and soul. Knew what I wanted more than anyone ever had. The black dress cinched around my body matched the black diamond wedding ring on my finger. The new band a mirror to the engagement ring. Somehow, he'd picked out something I wanted more than even I had imagined. I'd never even seen a black diamond until there was one on my finger.

"You're mesmerized," he said, loosening the bow tie at his neck.

"It's beautiful."

We'd spent the last couple of hours with our friends and Blake's family. It was nontraditional and somehow utterly perfect. We all had dinner at the five-star restaurant on the property. They'd closed down for the evening just for us, and we were served personally by the chef—a native Mescalero Apache Tribesman who infused his cultural cuisine with quintessential Southwestern flavors that were to die for.

Then, Ivy brought out a cake from a local bakery. The thing was a two-tier chocolate confection that I could barely keep from stuffing my mouth full. It was divine. We were going to have to take some home because I couldn't just eat it once.

After that, Tawa returned to the piano, and we had our first dance.

But the whole thing had been chill. No big spectacle. No bouquet toss. Nothing fancy. Which meant it was perfect in every way for us.

Now, we were headed upstairs to our honeymoon suite. Chase had the key clutched in his hand. I could tell he'd been ready to go for a while, but I'd wanted to savor the day as long as possible.

"A secret for a secret," he asked, taking my hand in his.

"You're my husband."

"That's not a secret."

"Yes, it is," I said, wrapping my arms around his neck.

"Fine. I accept it."

"What's your secret?"

The elevator dinged open, and he lifted me off of my

feet, sweeping my legs out from under me and carrying me down the hall.

"You'll see."

He tapped the card against the door and toed it open before carrying me across the threshold. I giggled at the symbolism behind it and pressed a kiss to his cheek, but when we were inside, my laughter faded, and awe replaced it.

"Oh my God," I whispered as he dropped me back to my feet.

The entire room was alight with candlelight. Hundreds of candles illuminating the massive honeymoon suite. Rose petals littered the floor from the door all the way to the king-size bed. A bottle of champagne was on ice, and a tray of chocolate-covered strawberries rested next to it. Two flutes were already filled and bubbling gently.

I could hear...water coming from another room. I grabbed a glass of champagne and followed the noise to find a Jacuzzi on the balcony of the bedroom. The jets were at full blast, and across the balcony was a sign that read, *Just married.*

"You did this?"

Chase wrapped an arm around my waist. "I might have had some help, but yes."

"It's incredible."

"As are you."

I laughed softly. I might have made him wait for me last night, but the anticipation had only grown. Seeing him waiting for me with wide, worshipful eyes at the end of the aisle had done something to me I couldn't explain.

Hearing the words *man and wife* had made my insides turn to goo. And now, we were here in this huge, momentous place at this exact time, and I was...shy?

Chase pressed a kiss to my neck. "What are you thinking?"

"Nothing."

He scoffed. "I can practically hear you thinking."

"It's nothing. Just, you know, the most anticipated night of sex of our lives."

He kissed my neck again. "You were the one who made me anticipate it. We could have had sex last night."

"Yeah, but..."

"You wanted to wait," he finished. "That's fine. And we don't have to have sex right now."

I half-turned to look at him skeptically. "Since when don't you want to have sex with me?"

"Oh, I want to," he said with a laugh. "And I'm going to, but we have *all night*. I have all night to ravish my wife."

I shivered at that word. "Wife."

"That's right. You're my wife. I want to take my time with you. I want all of you. And I don't want any nervous anticipation. Only excited anticipation of all the screaming orgasms I'm going to give you."

I laughed. "So sure of yourself."

"Tell me I shouldn't be."

I couldn't do that, of course. He knew exactly how to tease my body. So, I turned into him and stood on my tiptoes to claim his lips. But he wasn't in a hurry. He stood by his words, just enjoying the taste of me. The slow tease of my tongue against his lips before he opened up and gently pressed his tongue against mine. I sighed as he moved in slow, gentle circles.

His fingers slid up my back until he found the little pearl button that held the top of my wedding dress in place. He flipped it open, breaking the kiss with a smile.

"Subtle," I said breathlessly.

"Let me get you out of this thing."

"It's a feat," I admitted. "I think it only fits because of the corset."

"I know my way around a corset."

I shot him a skeptical look, but he twirled his fingers until I faced away from him again. His hands went to the laces at the back. Bailey had pulled them as tight as humanly possible to fit my waist and hold the rest of the relatively heavy dress up. As soon as he plucked the bow, the whole thing began to loosen, and I took a deep breath.

"Oh," I whispered. "That feels much better."

"Just wait," he said as he continued to loosen the laces.

His fingers strummed down my spine, revealing every inch of my now-exposed back.

"Do you know how beautiful you looked today?"

"Tell me."

"Like sunlight after a year of darkness," he confessed.

I inhaled. "In my black dress, I was sunlight?"

"Precisely. It was so very you. I like you just the way you are."

He slipped the mesh off of my shoulders, placing a soft kiss on one side.

"I loved getting to see you in this stunning dress."

The sleeves fell away.

"And to see you out of it."

With the laces undone and the sleeves gone, the tulle skirt fell into a fluffy heap on the ground. I was now in nothing but my black thong and Doc Martens.

"That's better."

Then, he smacked my ass.

I yelped. "Chase!"

"Now, get your ass in that hot tub."

"Here I thought, you were going to ravish me," I teased.

"And who said I wasn't?"

I stepped out of the dress, shucking off my shoes to the side, and headed toward the hot tub. Chase snagged my thong.

"Uh-uh," he said. "This goes, too."

I jerked my attention to him. "You're still fully clothed."

"Not for long."

"Really? Skinny-dipping?"

"Take that thong off and show me your pretty pussy," he commanded.

I smirked at him. He wanted a show? Fine.

I slid the thong down over my ass for his viewing pleasure. Then, when it was on the floor, I bent down and tossed it to him. He caught it in one hand, but his eyes were still on me as I turned around and strode into the heated water, giving him just a glimpse of what he wanted before it disappeared under the water.

He tucked my thong in his pocket and continued to watch me as he took the same amount of time to undress as he'd taken to undress me. Which meant I got to watch as he threw his bow tie to the side. As he undid each individual button, revealing the rippling abdominals. His jacket was tossed onto a nearby chair, and the shirt followed. My eyes scanned the strong arms and chest and then down, down, down to the V that led to one of my favorite parts of him. He popped the button of his pants and let them fall to the ground. He kicked his shiny black shoes to the side and the pants with them.

Then, he hooked his thumbs into his boxer briefs and pulled them over the full length of his cock. I salivated at the sight of him at full mast, ready and waiting for me.

The boxers disappeared entirely, and then he strode toward me, entirely unbothered by his own nakedness. And really, that was how he should be, as he was fucking gorgeous, tan and muscled from hours out on the lake and in the pool.

I had never wanted him more.

When he was finally in the hot tub, his cock disappearing beneath the bubbly water, he held his hand out for me. "Come here."

I moved through the water, wanting nothing more than to sit in his lap and slide his cock inside of me. But he turned me around, sitting me on his knee. My legs parted to accommodate his leg until my pussy was sitting right on his leg.

His hands were moving in gentle, relaxing strokes along my back. Unperturbed by the fact that I was now straddling one powerful thigh and my pussy was pulsing to life at the friction. Or maybe he was unaware that I was turned on just from undressing. That sitting on his knee like this was sweet, blissful torture. Especially because there was a jet near enough to be aimed at where my pussy met his thigh.

I squirmed as the pressure built, barely conscious of the massage happening. I tried to focus there and not below, but it was difficult. He was rubbing my shoulders, interjecting that with long strokes up and down my back.

My nipples pebbled, pert and aching from the tension. He had to know what he was doing. The touches to my neck as he worked his wet hands along my skin. The slow move over my ass before going back up my sides, so close to my breasts and yet so tantalizing far away. I could imagine those hands on my breasts, between my legs, inside of me.

I closed my eyes, and a soft sigh escaped me. I was rocking on his knee now. Chasing that sweet friction to its inevitable end point.

"Is that what you need?" he breathed into my ear.

"Yes," I panted.

"What else do you need?"

I didn't stop my rocking. I just panted, "Touch me."

So, he continued his slow perusal, moving his hands up my stomach, over my ribs, and up to my breasts. I gasped at the first tweak of my nipple with his fingers. I arched back into him, riding his knee like it was his cock, unabashedly. He moved to the other nipple, massaging it in between his thumb and forefinger.

"Oh," I breathed.

He banded one arm around my middle, sliding me backward until my back was pressed against his chest. His cock jutted up between us, and I reached my hand backward to lazily stroke it. He let me as he used his other hand to find my clit.

"Keep riding me," he commanded.

I tipped my head back as I did what he'd said, shameless. I wanted his cock. I wanted his fingers. I wanted his mouth. But I hadn't realized that I would take whatever he would give me. Even this little bit of friction and his fingers on my clit to push me toward the edge.

"Please," I gasped.

He slipped his fingers between my pussy and his leg and slid them effortlessly up into me. I gasped at the feeling of him filling me. It wasn't enough, and yet I rode him like my life depended on it. I wanted this.

My orgasm hung like a hazy edge, just out of reach.

He must have known because, without a second thought, he lifted me and had me face the nearest jet. The full blast of it hit my clit. All at once, I saw stars, and I couldn't stop the scream that ripped from my throat as my climax hit hard and fast.

He turned me to face him as I clamped around his fingers. Then, he stole my orgasm, claiming it with his mouth and lips and teeth.

"Mine," he told me. "My wife."

"Yes," I breathed. "My husband."

22

CHASE

My wife tasted like sex.

I wanted to taste that on her every day for the rest of our lives. Having her want to climax so badly that she nearly came on my knee was the most beautiful fucking thing I'd ever seen.

Last night had been so fucking hard. I lay awake in bed, imagining her only a door away, naked in bed without me. I'd had to take it out on my poor dick just to get enough sleep to be functional. All I could think about was her body and how much I fucking missed her. Not just the sex, but *her*.

If there had been any more anticipation for this day, then I didn't know it. Which was why I'd wanted to start in the Jacuzzi to loosen her up. If I felt it, then she certainly did. I hadn't even planned to have it be sexual. But then she'd been riding my leg, and well, what was I supposed to do?

As she came down, I gently released her.

She laughed. "Well, that was...incredible."

"I could watch it all day. In fact, I want to watch it again."

"My turn to watch," she argued.

"I'll give you as many fucking orgasms as I want."

Before I could do anything about it, she was already scurrying out of the hot tub and heading into the bedroom. She giggled as her ass jiggled. "Nope. My turn," she said. "I'm going to get the candles and drip them down your abs toward your cock. Then, we'll see who can control their orgasm."

While that actually did sound appealing, I wasn't done with her.

I hopped out of the water and followed her as she darted for the candles flickering in the adjoining room. I grabbed her in the middle, tossing her slippery body over my shoulder.

She laughed and said, "Put me down."

"Wax play after your next orgasm. Unless you want the wax on *you*."

"I preferred the ice," she said.

I tossed her down gently onto the bed, and she landed on the fluff of down comforter. I grabbed her ankles and jerked her down closer to me. Then dropped to my knees and buried my face between her legs.

She was still sensitive from her previous orgasm and shuddered under the first swish of my tongue from her lips to her swollen clit.

"Oh God," she gasped.

The sound of her voice went straight to my cock. I was already straining for control. It was physically painful not to thrust into her and take what I needed. But it was our wedding night, and we would have enough time for everything we both wanted. Candle wax and all if she preferred.

I was circling her clit so roughly that she was clutching the comforter and mewling, trying to get away from the pressure. But I didn't let up, not until she shuddered under me and released her second orgasm into my mouth.

"Fuck," I whispered at the sweet taste of her.

Her legs were trembling as I slid my hands up them to get a good look at the euphoria on her face. She opened her eyes and smiled in a crooked half-smile.

"Now, candles?" she teased.

"Now, I'm going to get inside of you."

Her eyes drifted to my straining cock. Pre-come dripped from the tip, and the veins popped from exertion.

"That sounds like a good call. Look at you."

"Dying for you," I admitted.

She lifted her arms over her head. "However you want me."

"In that case..."

I grasped her hips and flipped her over. She got onto all fours, swishing her pert ass in my direction. I seized it in my hands to hold her in place. Then, I slid them down over her wet pussy and between her legs. She groaned as I moved away from her clit, spreading her legs wider for me.

Once I had her at the right angle, I pressed the tip of my cock against her opening. Her moans increased in intensity, and she shifted backward. I smacked her ass, and she stopped moving. Then, I did it again because I loved the way it bounced. With my other hand on my cock, I ran it up and down the wet slickness of her. Not quite inside of her, but enough to get it nice and soaked.

"Tease," she muttered, dropping to her elbows.

But I wasn't teasing. I could barely hold myself back.

So, I decided not to.

I thrust forward, hard and fast, into her awaiting cunt. Tight and warm and wet. Like a fucking siphon for my balls, and there was nothing I wanted at all more than this in that moment.

I slowly slid back out of her and then thrust home again. Watching her ass move and her body jerk forward from my cock was hypnotic. I wasn't going to hold out much longer. I was already so fucking turned on. And the feel of her was my undoing.

"Harley," I grunted.

"I'm close," she told me, as if reading my mind.

I pumped into her harder, gripping her hips for dear life. I rammed into her until my pace turned brutal. I could barely contain myself to stop from fucking impaling her. And she was clamping down so good. Taking everything I was throwing at her.

Then, she stiffened, and her pussy contracted all around me.

That triggered everything in me, and I came with her, roaring my approval into the night.

I was dead. She'd slain me. My beautiful queen taking every single thing.

"I love you," I said as I came down, retreating from her body.

She dropped forward limply, and I drew her against me on the bed.

She cuddled into me, pressing her lips to my throat. "I love you, too."

I held her tight as euphoria settled over me. This was our wedding night. The culmination of all our desperate yearning.

Now, she was my wife.

And I was her husband.

And we would never be parted.

***

Candle wax littered the bedroom from our exploits. We'd showered it off, but the cleaning staff was probably not going to be pleased. Oh well.

I kissed my wife's messy hair. "You look beautiful."

"I'm a wreck."

"You're my wreck."

She yawned. "Why are we awake? It's so early."

I laughed. "I think it's noon."

"Oh," she whispered. "That sounds like a problem."

"Not for us. We don't have anywhere to be for a while. You got off work, and so did I. I'm just waiting to hear from the board about what they're going to say to my father. I should probably find my phone," I said, shifting out of the bed.

She reached for me with a whine. "Wait!"

"I'll be right back."

"But no work!"

"Soon, baby girl," I promised.

She huffed but lay back in the bed again and closed her eyes. I bet she'd be asleep in a few minutes anyway. We'd barely gotten a handful of hours of sleep.

I found my phone in my discarded suit coat after sliding into boxers. My battery was dead. I grumbled and found a charger in the room to attach it to. After a minute, the thing beeped.

And then didn't stop beeping for several minutes.

"What the hell?"

"What's that noise?" Harley asked with another yawn.

"My phone."

"Something happen?"

"I'm trying to figure that out."

I had a few dozen text messages, voicemails, and missed calls. Jesus. Had everyone found out that we'd eloped? Were they losing their shit?

Harley couldn't know about this. I wanted to shield her from any negativity for as long as I could. We'd have to plan a honeymoon for some time later, but I wanted to enjoy the rest of our day off and stay away from the rest of the world.

Unfortunately, the world had other plans.

When I listened to the first voicemail, my stomach dropped. I barely made it through the next, and by the last one, I was shaking. I scanned the text messages in a haze. Oh fuck.

"Harley, we have to go."

She sat up in the bed, holding the covers over her body. "What? Go where?"

"Home."

"Why? What happened?"

"My father."

Her eyes widened. "What did he do?"

"What didn't he do?" I asked. I tossed the phone to her, opened to the text messages I'd received from the board this morning while I was snuggled up with my new wife. "It turns out, there are about thirty women stepping forward with sexual assault allegations."

Harley's mouth dropped open. "Oh my God! That's horrible."

"Yeah. They date back to the '90s and go up to only a year ago. Some of them even said they tried to complain to HR before and were quietly let go. It seems that what happened with Eve and Dayna was just one of many, and being *willing* was apparently a rarity."

Harley winced. "Fuck."

"Pretty much."

"My mother called to tell me about it, too. She had heard about some of the rumors, but my dad always played it off as lies. Until they all came forward, that is."

"They were all telling the truth, but no one believes women," Harley said. "Women literally get *nothing* from these allegations, except hate. Why would we come forward if it wasn't true?"

She was so right. And I felt terrible for every single one of them.

"What are you going to do?" she asked.

"Get us home and find out where we go from here."

23

CHASE

We didn't go home first.

If I had to cut the day after my wedding short, fine, but I wasn't going to be without my wife. We dropped off Bailey. She asked to be informed as to what was going on. I just couldn't leave Harley out of this. She was everything to me, and she deserved to be at my side through this.

I'd spoken to Joseph, who was on the board, on the way back into town. He'd set up a meeting that afternoon to discuss how to move forward.

My father had been sacked.

From his own company.

I still couldn't believe it.

After everything that had happened with Dayna, I'd thought he could get away with murder. The man was infallible. He always had been.

And yet something had finally felled the giant.

I hated that this was what had done it. I'd known he was a monster. But I hadn't really known how bad it was.

I was glad that the company had moved with decisive action to get him out of there. It should have happened long ago.

I navigated into the parking lot and took my regular spot at the front. Harley's legs were kicked up on the dash. Her head was buried in a thriller that she'd started on the back from Ruidoso. She looked up at me over the edge and grinned.

"Hey, handsome," she said.

"Are you sure you don't want to drive home?"

I wanted her there, but I didn't want her to have to deal with any of this either. It was a conundrum. One that I still couldn't quite reconcile.

"We've not been married twenty-four hours. In no way am I going home without you."

"I don't want you to leave," I said, reaching for her hand. She stuck a finger into the book and dropped it into her lap. "But you don't have to come inside either. This is Sinclair business."

"And I'm a Sinclair now."

My heart warmed at those words. "I love to hear that."

"You're also a Wright," she teased.

I laughed. "Fair."

"Look, it's going to be fine. Your dad has already left the building. You're just doing next steps. But I can go if you want me to?"

"No," I said quickly. "That's not what I mean."

"I can sit in the car," she said with an arched eyebrow. "I'd planned to read this book, overlooking the mountains, you know?"

"We'll go back," I promised her.

"We'd better."

"I owe you a honeymoon, too."

"I can't wait." Her eyes went distant, as if envisioning what was to come. "Now, go have your meeting so we can go home sooner and do it."

I snorted. "Do it?"

She arched an eyebrow. "So you can fuck me?"

"And I absolutely will," I said. "But you can't sit out here. It's too hot today to read in the car."

"I'll be fine."

"Harley, it's over a hundred. I don't know how long this is going to take. Hopefully quick, but you never know. Why don't you sit in my office and read while I'm in my meeting?"

"All right. You convinced me," she agreed easily, slipping from my grasp and exiting the car.

I took a deep breath. Well, here goes nothing.

Harley was waiting with her thriller in hand as I came around to the front of the car. I took her hand in mine again, and we headed into Sinclair Realty. I'd been working here for years and known my whole life that I wanted to take over the company. With the prospect of doing that today, my heart was skittering in my chest. I couldn't decide if it was nerves or anticipation or something else. Only that I hadn't wanted to take over because of this. Just like I hadn't wanted to become the face of the company because of my father's affair.

He had a way of wrecking all of my carefully laid plans. Apparently, he did that with everyone.

Harley's Docs were harsh against the marble tiles as

we crossed the lobby. Agents were milling around, chatting in groups about the turmoil in the company. Eyes followed us the whole way, widening in recognition at the woman at my side. To her credit, she was unfazed by the attention. Just smiled back and even gave a little wave to one woman who was openly gawking at us.

"They really seem interested in us," she said once we were in the elevator on the way to the top floor.

"Not every day a Wright steps into Sinclair Realty."

She shrugged. "Corporate takeover," she said with a wink. "I'm starting at the top and working my way down."

"Ah, is that what you consider this?" I asked as I pulled up her left hand and gestured to the ring on it.

"Damn straight."

I laughed, loving that she could bring levity to the situation. As if she knew precisely how bad my nerves were. And she probably did. Harley knew me better than anyone and always had.

"Ready?" she asked me as we neared the top floor.

I nodded. "It's going to be fine."

"Chase…"

"I can do this."

"I know you can, but it's a big step." She took my chin in her hand and tipped my face down to hers. "You're in control here. Don't forget that."

I pressed a harsh kiss to her mouth. "How did I get so lucky?"

"You came to a Wright wedding."

"Luck indeed."

I took her hand in mine just as the elevator opened to the top floor to chaos. We both froze in surprise at the mess of people standing on the landing, arguing. Almost the entire board was there, shouting at each other...along with my *sister*?

I cleared my throat. "What's going on here?"

The room quieted as I stepped forward. Ashleigh paled at my appearance, her eyes shooting to Harley. We hadn't spoken since she'd tried to fuck with my relationship. She'd tried to reach out, but I just didn't have it in me to deal.

I didn't exactly want to deal with her right now either, but she was probably shaken up by what we'd learned about Dad. She worked at the company, too, and she'd been more on Dad's side than I ever had been. She hardly approved of his extramarital affairs, but this was next level.

By her red-rimmed eyes and, dare I say, disheveled appearance, she hadn't known any of it either. And was just as hurt as Mom and I had been by the news.

"Chase," she said with relief in her voice, "you made it."

"I made it," I agreed.

"And you brought Harley."

"That's right."

Ashleigh swallowed, wariness in her expression. "The board says that I can't be in the meeting."

"Why would you be in the meeting?"

Her jaw clenched. "What do you mean, why? *I'm* a Sinclair, too. I've worked at the company longer than you. I have a controlling stake. I should be involved in the decision-making." She lifted her chin. "After all, I was the one who convinced the women to come forward about Dad."

I stilled at those words. *Ashleigh* had turned on Dad. She'd found out what was going on and helped make it public. I couldn't believe it. I'd only seen my sister as the manipulative, conniving thing that she was. How she always liked to dip her fingers into anything with gossip and stir the pot. Was that what this was? Did she want to have a bigger role in the company and couldn't get it any other way?

"You broke the news about his sexual harassment allegations?"

"I've been working on it for *months*," she said, her voice tight. "No one wanted to come forward because they didn't think anyone would believe them."

"Why didn't you tell me?"

She chewed on her lip. Her eyes darting to Harley and back. "You were still on his side."

I barely managed to keep a laugh from exploding out of me. Since when had I ever been on Dad's side? Was that what she'd thought all this time? That because I had been chosen as the face of the company that I wanted to be on his good side?

"That's why you hid her, right?" Ashleigh asked.

"No," I said. "Harley has nothing to do with any of this. I wasn't on his side. You could have told me about this."

"I guess I should have. I'm used to working alone," she admitted. For a moment, her voice went soft, like I was getting a glimpse of my real sister. The one I'd known before the world hardened her. I hadn't believed that she was underneath all of this. "I've been managing him for years. That's why I was always in his space. As you jokingly called me his assistant." Her words held venom—and maybe rightfully so. "I didn't know how bad it was until more recently. I just knew that employees weren't comfortable around him."

"Most men don't see it," Harley said softly at my side. "You've never had to be on your guard the way we have."

Ashleigh tipped her head at Harley. "It's second nature."

I sighed. I hated that they were right. I hadn't looked deeper, and I should have. At what Ashleigh was doing and why. At my father's exploits. At all of it.

"All right," I said with a nod. "Come to the meeting."

"Sir," Joseph said, "are you sure about this?"

Joseph was my favorite board member. He'd been at my side through all of this with my father. From his relationship with Dayna and on. He wasn't sure about Ashleigh. And to be honest, I wasn't sure about her either. Not after everything she'd done. But in this, with Harley's nod of approval, I felt like I was in the right. I could at least hear her out. She'd been hurt by the monster we called Father as much or even more than I had.

"Yes, I'm sure. Shall we convene in the conference room?" I said, taking control of the chaotic office space.

"Of course," Joseph said.

He gestured to the remaining board members, and they began to file toward the conference room.

His eyes landed on Harley, and he held his hand out.

"Joseph Johnson. You must be Harley Wright. We've heard a great deal about you recently."

She grinned and took his hand. "All good things, I hope."

"Not exactly, but I'm sure Chase will correct us about all of that."

She laughed. "I bet he will."

Joseph smiled down at her. "Just keep him happy. It's going to be a rough couple of weeks."

"I plan to keep *her* happy," I interjected.

She lifted her book. "By reading in his office while y'all have your big, important meeting. Don't worry. I don't want to be involved." She fluttered the book and turned to me. "Have fun at your little shindig."

I shook my head and kissed her. "Love you."

"Love you, too."

I'd just released her and gestured to Ashleigh to fall into step next to me when the elevator dinged again.

My gaze shifted to Joseph. "Were we waiting on someone else?"

He shook his head. "Just you, sir."

The doors opened, and my father took up the doorway like the giant he was. An unkempt, greasy mess, but a giant nonetheless.

He took one look at me and Ashleigh, clearly colluding side by side, and his fury burned. Before finding Harley still standing in the open space. And then he exploded.

"Who let that Wright *whore* in my building?" he snarled.

24

HARLEY

W*hore.*

How eloquent.

I rolled my eyes. "Ugh. This guy again?"

Chase barely suppressed a laugh as he left his sister's side to come stand next to me. He put his hand in mine, a unit. And I was glad for it.

Arnold Sinclair was not supposed to be here today. That was part of the reason Chase had hustled to get back. The board had dealt with his dad, and now, they were moving on. How had Arnold even found out about the board meeting? Did he have someone sympathetic to his cause within the ranks?

It wouldn't surprise me. He'd worked at the company for years. Inherited it from his father and all that. The way Chase was inheriting it from him. I didn't know what he thought he would accomplish by showing up here.

"Dad, you need to leave," Chase said.

"No one can make me leave my own property," he snarled.

"In fact, Arnold," Joseph began, "we already made you leave. Don't make us call security to escort you out."

Arnold shook his head. "After all these years, Joseph, you're going to turn against me."

"There are no sides here," Joseph said. "There is only right and wrong. What you did was wrong, and the company that you claim to love doesn't stand for it."

"Think about the women you hurt, Dad," Ashleigh said, finding her voice. "Think about how *they* felt when you hurt them and discarded them. Can't you think of anyone but yourself?"

"All of you just *believe* these women," he snarled. "Without any proof. My own flesh and blood crafting stories to get me out of the way."

Ashleigh flinched at the words hurled at her. I wanted to defend her, defend all the women, but arguing with Arnold was futile. He had no power here. He was exerting himself like he always did. The best thing to do in this situation was nothing. It was useless to deal with him when he was just manic.

"Enough," Chase said. "You're through, Dad. You need to leave."

"You aren't the CEO here."

"Maybe not. But neither are you. And the board has already decided to dismiss you based on the sheer volume of allegations."

"Bullshit." He pointed his finger at me. "You're just listening to your Wright. They're trying to ruin us, and you're letting them."

"You will not speak to Harley that way," he snapped.

"You're an idiot if you don't see that she's trying to

tear down everything we've built."

"You've already gone down this road, and I threatened to quit before letting you speak to her like that," he told his father with barely concealed fury in his voice. "I won't tolerate it anymore."

"You can fix this, Chase," his dad said as if he realized his behavior wasn't getting him anywhere. He stepped forward, pleading with Chase from a new angle. "You can make them see reason. Come on. I've always been in your corner. You can be CEO, and I can work where I've been this whole time. You aren't ready to run everything on your own."

Chase's face was like stone. "Is that what you believe?"

"You're brilliant at it. I raised you. I trained you. I know you can do the job, but you still need me. I've worked here too long." His father put on a spectacular show. Owen would have even been proud of the duplicity. "I know I said some things in anger at dinner, but I never wanted you out of the company."

"And Harley?"

He swallowed, but couldn't quite suppress his disgust. "I still stand that you can do better."

"Okay, Dad," Chase said softly. "Okay, you can have another chance."

Ashleigh and Joseph looked at him with disbelievingly. A word of protest was already on his sister's lips. Arnold looked triumphant.

But they hadn't been looking at Chase when he said it. They didn't see the way his lips twisted in displeasure. The way his eyes had hardened into gemstones and his resolve set. Arnold should have known it would never be this easy.

So, I wasn't surprised when Chase continued in a brisk, cutting manner with a dark smile on his lips, "If you apologize to my *wife*."

The room went deathly silent.

Arnold's face slackened in shock. Ashleigh's eyes darted to my hand, where the black diamond shone in brilliant clarity. Joseph coughed into his hand, as if he'd been about to laugh and covered it at the last minute.

"Wife," Arnold said flatly.

"That's right," Chase said.

"You're not married."

"We are," I said.

I held up my left hand, letting him get a better look at the diamond on my finger. The wedding band beside it. The one he'd slid onto my finger only last night. I'd thought we'd spend the next day lounging around our penthouse honeymoon suite, eating top-quality food, drinking champagne, and enjoying the benefits of the empty ski resort. Instead, we were here.

"Oh my God!" Ashleigh gushed. She rushed forward, throwing her arms around her brother. "Congratulations! When did this happen? Tell me everything!"

Chase laughed and pulled back from his sister. "We eloped yesterday in New Mexico. We went to Holliday Ski."

"You stayed at *my* chalet?" Arnold demanded.

"No," Chase drawled. "We stayed at the resort with Blake."

"You married a *Wright*?"

"Yes," Chase said.

"I'm a Sinclair now," I said with my chin tipped up. The words I'd uttered to Chase in the car coming back in full force.

Chase smiled. "And I'm a Wright."

"No," Arnold said. He shook his head, as if he couldn't face those words.

"It's done," Chase said.

"This is absurd. You can't marry her. Let alone without a prenup."

His eyes snapped between us like we were insane for what had happened. Maybe it had been a quick cere-mony decided at the last minute, but it didn't change our love for one another. Prenup or not.

"You can still annul it."

"Daddy, they're married," Ashleigh said.

"Accept it," I added.

"So, those are the terms," Chase said, lifting his chin. "You apologize to my wife for the horrid things you said about her, and you can have another chance."

Arnold's eyes were hard when they came to rest on his son. They weren't terms. There was no possibility that this man would apologize to *me*. The twenty-two-year-old harlot he thought had ensorcelled his son. The only reason Chase had offered it to him at all was because he knew that his dad would never do it.

"Never," he snarled, as I'd known he would. "This slut has twisted your mind."

"Joseph, call security, please," Chase said with a dismissive glance away from his father.

"Of course," Joseph said.

"How fucking dare you!" Arnold said.

"Come on, Harley. This meeting shouldn't take long," he said, holding his hand out to me.

But Arnold grasped his son by the collar. "You can't do this to me."

Chase moved me hastily behind him. "I've done nothing *to you*. You did all of this to yourself. These are the consequences to your actions. You might never admit your fault, but you did this. You ruined your position here. You hurt countless women. And you lost the love and support of your wife and children *all on your own*." Chase wrenched his suit out of his dad's hands just as security rushed out of the elevator. "And you will suffer those consequences for once."

"You need to come with us, Mr. Sinclair," one of the officers said, reaching for Arnold.

"Get your hands off me!" Arnold swore at the security guards. He swung backward to get out of their grip. The first guard secured his arms, and the other began to drag him backward. "You can't do this!"

"Good-bye, Dad," Chase said resolutely.

I put my hand into his as we watched his dad be dragged away while he ranted and raved. It was a sad sight, but also a welcome one. As Chase had said, he'd gotten what he deserved. Finally. At least someone had.

"Well, that was dramatic," Ashleigh said with an eye roll.

"Quite," Joseph agreed. "He always did have a flair for the dramatic."

Ashleigh laughed. "It runs in the family."

"You are quite dramatic," Chase agreed.

"Me?" She shot me a glance. "Y'all went and *eloped*!"

"We did," Chase said, and he kissed me again.

"Congratulations, by the way," Joseph said.

"Thank you," I said.

"I want to know all the details and why I wasn't a bridesmaid," Ashleigh said with a pointed look. "But can we finish this meeting first?"

"I believe that's in order," Chase agreed.

"If you don't mind, Mrs. Sinclair," Joseph said with a head nod in our direction, "I'd like to borrow your husband for a minute to vote him in as CEO."

I flushed at those words. *Mrs. Sinclair*. I wasn't changing my name—that was for damn sure—but that didn't mean I didn't like hearing it. I was his. *His*. And now, people knew. All that was left was to break the news to *my* family. Suddenly, I couldn't wait.

"I don't mind as long as you bring the CEO back to me in one piece," I teased. "I have plans for him tonight."

Ashleigh chortled.

Chase grinned down at me devilishly and slung me up into his arms. He kissed me hard. "I love you."

I laughed. "I love you, too."

"I cannot wait for these plans."

"Oh yeah? You don't even know what they are."

"I can guess," he said with a seductive look.

"How about telling my brothers?"

He put me back on my feet with a smile. "I can take a punch."

I snorted. "I was thinking of putting a family feud to an end."

"Let's do it."

25

HARLEY

"Ready?" Chase asked from the driver's side of his Porsche.

I sat on the passenger side, staring down at the diamond ring on my left hand. I still couldn't believe how stunning it was and that he'd picked out my dream ring without my input. I twirled it around and around and around. A new habit that I had no intention of breaking. I never wanted to take the beautiful thing for granted.

"Harley," he said softly.

I jerked my gaze up to meet his. I wasn't nervous. Not really. Not after what we went through to get where we were. But calling a meeting of all the Wrights at Wright Vineyard was a bold move. Maybe I should have done it another way, but I wasn't sure how.

"I'm ready."

"We don't have to tell everyone like this."

"I want everyone to know," I assured him.

"That's not in doubt."

"I want them to know *now*."

I'd already told Mom. I couldn't keep it from her another minute.

After Chase had officially been named CEO, we'd gone back to his—now, *our*—house, and I got on video chat to tell my mom. She was shocked and ecstatic. Though she had been sad that she hadn't been there to see her only daughter get married, I thought she had been a little happy that her rule follower had finally followed her heart and rebelled.

"Then, let's enter the lion's den together."

I nodded. "Together."

We stepped out of his car, and he came around to take my hand. The walk up the stone path that led to the front of the vineyard felt shorter than normal. As if we took one step and then another and we were instantly at the large barn door that stood ajar, ready and waiting for us.

He squeezed my hand for reassurance and pushed the door all the way open. Inside was a crowd of Wrights. I'd done this, and still, I was struck by how *much* family I had now. I'd been so used to it being so small that I sometimes forgot when I invited all the Wrights, it was *all* the Wrights.

Whitt and Eve were standing with West and Nora, who were thankfully back from their honeymoon and the end of the tour. The rest of Cosmere lounged in chairs nearby. Beyond that, Jordan and Julian had drinks in hand beside their co-owner, Hollin, and the girls— Annie, Jennifer, Piper, and Blaire. My cousins—Jensen, Austin, Landon, Morgan, and Sutton—were in a cluster in one corner. Jensen was pointing fingers at his siblings, and the rest seemed to be arguing in the genial way they did. Their significant others were scattered about the room, along with their kids and friends.

Jensen's eldest, Colton, had his head buried in his phone against a wall. A blonde stood at his side, staring up at him with longing in her eyes. They'd been on-again, off-again all year. This summer had been bumpier than ever. If it wasn't enough that he was Harvard bound in a week's time, there had been a horrible accident at the old train tracks, and one of their friends had died.

Understandably so, Colton had seemed off ever since. I didn't blame him if he wanted to cut all ties to Lubbock and make a new name for himself in Cambridge, away from the legacy of the Wrights.

Honestly, sometimes, it was still strange to think that I wouldn't be going with him. But I knew I'd made the right choice.

"Surprise!" I said, holding our hands up to the crowd.

The room quieted, turning toward us. All eyes were suddenly on us. Everyone wondering exactly why I'd called them here. Now, the moment of truth.

I caught Chase's eye, and his smile warmed me. This was it. This was the right thing to do. No more hiding. Not ever again.

"Thank you so much for coming on short notice. I know it's a lot to get all of the family together. We're quite a bunch, aren't we?"

They looked around at each other, chuckling at how much we'd grown over the years.

"Chase and I have an announcement to make."

"But before we do," Chase interjected, "I'd like to request that no Wrights punch me."

More laughter from everyone. Eyes turning to Jordan, who just shrugged. Annie rolled her eyes at him. Julian slugged him in the arm.

"Hey!" Jordan said. Then another shrug. "He earned it."

"What's this about?" Whitt asked. He stepped forward, his face going white, as if he realized the news before it was announced.

"It's okay," Eve said. Her eyes were shining with tears of excitement. Bailey was at her side, and she must have already spilled the beans to her sister. "Let her speak."

"Harley?" West said.

I turned my left hand to face my family. "Chase and I got married."

There was a moment of deafening silence. Not whatever they must have been anticipating. Something more permanent. Something they hadn't been included in.

I opened my mouth, prepared to defend our choice and tell them that they could all go to hell if they didn't agree. We hadn't done this for them. I was young, but not *that* young. Not anymore. This was what we wanted. What we'd fought for.

But the moment before I could speak, Eve, Bailey, and Annie rushed forward. A din of, "Congratulations!" followed as the girls smothered me with hugs and excitement.

I laughed at the sheer volume of their enthusiasm. My brothers stood on the periphery, but I couldn't see what they were doing, and I didn't know what they were thinking. Only that my family was happy for us. Wrights and Sinclairs were together, and they were *happy*.

"I was there," Bailey declared excitedly. "It was a beautiful ceremony."

"I cannot believe you didn't invite me!" Annie said. She pushed Chase, and he laughed, and then she threw her arms around him. "Married! My best friend is married. I'm so fucking happy for you."

"Thanks, Annie."

"Pissed, mind you. I should have been there." She pointed her finger at him.

"I know, but we wanted it to be for us."

"We can have a big reception here, and everyone will be invited," I promised her. "I really want to wear my wedding dress again."

Annie giggled. "I bet."

"It was black!" Bailey told everyone.

"I have pictures," I told them, pulling out my phone to show the dress and the few pictures I had from the ceremony. Ivy had had a photographer there, but we wouldn't get the official pictures back for weeks. I only had a sneak peek picture that I showed off to the girls.

They took the phone and oohed and aahed appropriately.

My cousins stepped up, offering their own congratulations. Many of them understanding the desire for an elopement over a big ceremony. Except West's wife, Nora, of course.

"I'm a wedding planner," she said with a pout. "I wanted to help."

"You can plan the reception. I mean, honestly, would you plan the reception? I'd love that so much."

"Yes! I am so doing that for you." Nora glanced back at West. My brothers were still hanging back, looking at each other in shock. "Give them a minute. They'll come around."

"Thanks, Nor."

"I'll cut them if they don't get their asses over here soon," Annie promised.

Eve nodded. "A hundred percent."

But that wasn't necessary. Once my Wright cousins cleared out, my brothers stepped forward as a unit. Chase straightened under the eyes of Jordan, Julian, Whitton, and Weston, prepared to take another punch. His joke had only been half a joke anyway. We had no idea how they would respond. We just hoped they'd accept it.

"You're happy?" Whitt asked.

I nodded. "Beyond happy."

"And this is what you want?"

I slid my hand into Chase's. "This is where I belong."

"Then, I'm happy for you." Whitt drew me into a hug, and I melted into my brother.

West jumped in next, throwing his arms around both of us. "I'm happy, too," he declared. "Though it seems a touch fast."

"Mom said I'm in my rebellious era."

West snorted. "It's about time," he said at the same time Whitt said, "Isn't that every era?"

They glanced at each other and laughed. Twins.

"Like mother, like daughter," I offered.

"Well, I, for one, think you could do better," Jordan said as he held his hand out for Chase.

"Fair," Chase said.

"You're not changing your name, right?" Jordan asked. He wrinkled his nose. "I don't know if I could call you Harley Sinclair."

"What about Chase Wright?" I teased.

Jordan's eyes rounded. "Is it possible I like that less?"

"We're not changing our names," Chase told him with a headshake. "Don't worry your little head."

"Maybe we'll hyphenate!" I dared.

Julian laughed. "You would, wouldn't you?"

"Harley Sinclair-Wright has a ring to it," Chase agreed.

"You mean, Wright-Sinclair," I fired back.

"Whatever you like, dear."

"That's the right answer," Julian muttered under his breath.

"Anyway, it's all to say that the family feud is over," I let my brothers know. "Arnold is sacked from Sinclair Realty. He's not part of the business anymore. Ashleigh actually helped take him down."

Julian's eyes widened. "Ashleigh did that?"

I nodded. "Couldn't have happened without her. Look, neither side is perfectly innocent, but I want this to end. Chase is the new CEO at Sinclair Realty. He's my husband. Let's put the past behind us."

"I will if you will," Chase said to my brothers.

Whitt and West shrugged at each other. Julian crossed his arms, clearly lost in thought about Ashleigh's involvement. But it was Jordan who finally laughed.

"If anyone could do this, it's you, Harley." He pulled me into a hug. "I'm happy for you."

"You are?" I whispered, tears in my eyes.

Jordan took a step back and raised his voice. "Let's give a cheer for the newlyweds! The Wright-Sinclairs!"

The crowd roared their approval. Everyone was applauding and going wild, yelling for us. A tear tracked down my cheek at the love from my family. Even my brothers, who had hated Chase so much at the beginning of all of this. It was amazing that we'd ever made it this far. That we were here right now.

Chase slid his hand around my waist. "A toast to my wife."

"For my husband," I breathed.

He smiled. "Might as well give them a show, huh?"

"Chase!"

But he was already turning me in place, dipping me low to the ground. A burst of laughter escaped me as I stared up into my husband's bright blue eyes. They were full of adoration. Like he'd never seen anything he wanted more in the entire world. And I was that something.

Years of pining.

Months of yearning.

Weeks of longing.

Days of need.

Had all led to this moment here—forever.

EPILOGUE
HARLEY

Four Months Later

Fall was just blowing into Lubbock. Reluctantly brushing off the ninety-degree weather with easy seventies while the leaves turned crimson, squash orange, and mustard yellow. And I was in my black wedding dress in front of the vineyard.

"I will never get tired of seeing you in that dress," Chase said. His hands moved to my hips, drawing me in closer. "Or out of it."

"The reception hasn't even started, and you're already talking about getting me naked."

He arched an eyebrow. "There is nothing wrong with wanting my wife naked underneath me."

"Or on top of you."

"Or bent over," he agreed. "Whatever position you prefer, baby girl."

"All of them."

"I'm convinced."

"Y'all ready?" Nora called as she strode toward us in her mile-high heels. I still didn't know how she navigated them like a pro. "Everything is set."

I kicked one Doc Marten–covered foot out from under the floof of my dress. "We're ready."

"We could use fifteen more minutes," Chase said at the same time.

I lifted my brows. "Filthy."

"I'm going to pretend I didn't hear that so I don't have to hide anything from West," Nora said with a laugh.

"We've been married for months. He knows we've had sex, right?"

"We had sex years before that," Chase added under his breath.

"Uh-uh-uh, do not need to know," Nora said with a laugh. "Let's get you into your reception."

"We're ready," I said again.

Chase took my hand in his and pressed a kiss to the knuckles. "We are."

We followed Nora to the entrance to the Wright Vineyard barn. We'd agreed to have the reception here with both of our families, fathers excluded, even though we could have gone with neutral territory.

We'd stuck to it—the Wright-Sinclair feud was over.

Our fathers might be trying to hang on to it, but we were done. Arnold was out of Chase's life and dealing with the aftermath of being taken to court for his sexual harassment cases. I was personally rooting for the girls to win and take him for everything. Chase and I didn't need his money.

Even better, my mom had left Owen.

She was waiting for us at the closed barn doors. She pressed a kiss to my cheek. "So proud of you, honey."

"So glad to have you here."

"Glad I finally made the move."

Oh yeah, and she'd moved to Lubbock to be with her kids. Grandma and Grandpa had reluctantly come, too, and were now in a home down the street from Mom's new house. She could walk there every morning to check on them for a fraction of the cost of where they'd been in Seattle. It was the best of all worlds.

"Me too."

She hugged Chase. "My wonderful son-in-law."

"Anything for you, Tanya."

"And for me?" Charlotte Sinclair asked as she took up the other side of our set.

"Of course, Mom."

We'd compromised on our entrance. Since no one else had been invited to our elopement, we'd wanted our moms to walk us into our reception. Let them have the moment we'd denied them four months earlier. As strange as the pair were—a former groupie and a trophy wife—they'd become friends. Maybe because my mom had just moved into town and Chase's mom was freshly divorced. They had more in common than they'd ever known.

"Let's do this," Nora proclaimed.

The doors opened. I took Chase's hand in mine and looped my arm through my mom's. Then, the four of us were striding inside to the announcement, "Mr. and Mrs. Wright-Sinclair!"

The room was crowded with Wrights, but also

Sinclair friends and family as well. It was nice to see it was full of all the people in our lives. Ashleigh with her new boyfriend, Matthew. The first guy she'd ever really been herself with. I was happy for them. Kai and Elsie with her pregnant belly. My work friends clustered around Courtney in her wheelchair. Blake and Ivy Holliday, all the way in from New Mexico. Bailey still wouldn't tell me what was going on with them, but I'd get it out of her sometime.

I kissed my mom's cheek. "I love you."

"Love you, too, sweetie."

Chase released his own mom, and then we were on the empty dance floor. I'd chosen our opening song—an instrumental version of "Ziggy Stardust"—and the first notes made Chase laugh.

"Of course. It's our song."

"Not quite the same without Bowie's lyrics, but I wanted something we could show off to."

And show off we did.

Because we'd spent the last four months in ballroom dancing classes. Chase's love for dancing had taken me by surprise, and when I'd suggested that we learn to dance together, he'd been above and beyond excited. Now, we were in classes every week, and I didn't see it stopping just because the reception was over. I still stumbled compared to his smooth steps, but I was getting better.

The crowd cheered our moves. Not quite choreographed as I followed Chase through all the steps we'd learned over the last couple of months. My confidence growing the longer we were out there. Until I was smiling and twirling and enjoying myself in a way that I'd never known I could off the ice.

At the end of the song, Chase dipped me to a round of applause. I laughed and leaned up to steal a kiss.

"I have another surprise for you," I whispered against his lips.

His eyes lit up. "What's that?"

The music changed.

Chase burst into laughter. "You're joking!"

He whipped me up to my feet just as the opening of ABBA's "Dancing Queen" played through the speakers. I could still remember that first night we'd shared together all those years ago. How this song played through his speakers and we danced like fools around his living room. He lifted me into his arms, twirling me in place. Then, I slid down his front, and sparks had leaped to life every place we touched.

"I thought you'd like it."

"I love it," he confirmed.

And then we were dancing our asses off. Our friends and family joined in the mayhem. All of us singing the song at the top of our lungs and dancing like no one was watching. It was a joyous, heartfelt moment. A bit of nontraditional in the middle of our very traditional reception.

We moved from there to dinner—a plated three-course meal from a caterer that Nora swore by. It was one of the best meals of my life. Almost as good as the restaurant we'd eaten at in New Mexico for our wedding night. I'd asked Nora to limit the toasts, but somehow, that memo hadn't gotten around to my family.

After Bailey and Annie gave a toast for each of us, other members of our families stood up and began to speak for us. The words that flowed was like a balm for my soul. A fresh spring in an empty desert. Watching all the people who were my entire world not just accept me and Chase, but also prove that this was the union they believed in meant the world.

I had to swipe tears from my eyes by the end of it. Chase squeezed my hand under the table. A smile on his face.

We had cake, and I threw my bouquet. I even let Chase dig up my skirts for the black garter Bailey and I had picked out for the moment. His wicked smile when he reached for it only made me more excited for the night to come.

And then we danced.

And danced.

And danced.

We danced so long that my feet ached and sweat beaded my pale skin and joy filled my entire being.

Chase grasped my hand, tugging me out of the spotlight and off of the dance floor. "A secret for a secret?"

I grinned. "You first!"

"Someone is stealing my wife," he said with a raised eyebrow as he tugged me out of the barn and into the night air.

"*You're* stealing your wife," I said. "That isn't a secret."

"All right. I have one." He faced me, walking backward toward the vineyard. "I booked our honeymoon."

My eyes lit up. "Without me?"

"You couldn't decide."

"Rude."

He laughed. "You're going to like it."

"Are you going to tell me where we're going?"

"A castle in the Scottish Highlands."

"What?" I gasped. "Really? A whole fucking castle?"

"Yep. And you can read as many thrillers as you want and drink my hot chocolate and wander the wilderness in your Doc Martens."

"We'd better have a huge bed."

"Of course. Because I will be fucking you every night in it."

I laughed and threw myself into his arms. "I can't wait! Can we sneak down to London? I want to take you to all of my favorite places."

"Yes. You think I planned to take you there and not get to go to all the places in London that you taunted me with when you were on study abroad."

I grinned. "This is the perfect surprise."

"You owe me a secret, you know?"

"Well, I was going to show this to you later, but I think now works."

I reached into the folds of my skirt for the pocket that had been added to my tulle skirt now that I'd had enough time for alterations. I removed a piece of paper and passed it to him.

He took it and searched the words in the moonlight.

His eyes snapped up to mine. "It's official?"

"Wright-Sinclair."

"For both of us?"

I nodded.

He swept me up into his arms. We swung in a circle,

and a giggle escaped me. He set me gently back on my feet. His hand went to my face, tilting it up to his.

"Now, we're the same. No more family differences at all."

"I like it. I never thought I'd change my name."

"Well, I certainly didn't," he said with a laugh. "But it's only fair that we both do."

"Then, our children will have the same name."

His eyes widened. "Children?"

"*Not* another secret," I assured him. "But one day…"

"One day," he agreed.

We came to the bench where we had been together all those months earlier. The time when we had come out about our relationship to our entire family, and now, we were in the same place again, but everything had irrevocably changed. And it was all for the better.

This was what we had been leading toward.

A life where we had saved both of our families and created a new one in the process.

A life worth living with the person worth living it with.

The End

WHAT'S COMING NEXT?

CATCH A KING
(Dorset & King, #1)

Malcolm King is my next contemporary romance. He and Arden Rivers are a fiery pair.

Think: arranged marriage, fake dating, oil dynasty, (more) rival families, chronic illness rep, and one HUGE Texas family.

Turn the page to read chapter one!

CATCH A KING
CHAPTER 1

Arden

The last box didn't fit in the truck.

It was hard not to see this as a metaphor for my life.

"Come on, Arden," Grayson said, reaching for the box in my arms. "You don't have to go."

I glared at him as I stepped backward. "Don't fucking touch me."

"You shouldn't be carrying anything that heavy."

"Oh so *now* you care about my symptoms?" I asked, my voice laced with heavy sarcasm.

I set the box on the back of my truck, opened the front door and slid the final box into the passenger's seat. It was piled three high and was probably a danger to my safety if I got into an accident, but at least it was done.

Nine long months later, I was finally *officially* divorced and moving home. Rivers Ranch, here I come!

I slammed the passenger door shut and ignored Grayson as he trailed me around to the driver's side. It had been torture to the nth degree to live in the same house with him over the last couple months, but I'd had too much debt to rent my own place. Denver was rapidly growing out of everyone's price point.

"What happens if you have an episode when you're on the road?" Grayson asked.

"Gray, if you gave a single fuck about me, you wouldn't have pushed me away while I was in the hospital and then spent my dad's money on gambling and hookers in Vegas." I wrenched the door open, nailing him in the side. He grunted and stepped back. "I don't know why you think I give a flying fuck what you think."

"I'm worried about you, Arden." He reached forward as if to tuck a loose strange of my blonde hair behind my ear. I veered out of his way.

"Don't care. I didn't care when I divorced you. I certainly don't care now."

"Baby..."

"Don't call me that. Don't call me anything. Better yet, don't call. Forget I existed, because that's my plan, Gray. I'm hoping to forget any of this ever happened."

"You don't mean that."

"I don't know how to get this into your head. I'm leaving. I'm not your baby. I'm not anything to you anymore. Just someone that you used to know."

His face hardened at those words. I always knew when I struck home because it was right before he got mean. And I wasn't having that today.

I cut him off before he could say anything else, "It's a ten hour drive home and I don't have any time for you or your bullshit."

I sank into the driver's seat and slammed the door shut. Grayson was yelling something through the glass, but I just turned the truck on and blasted the stereo system, drowning out his pathetic tirade.

Good riddance, Grayson Harris.

Pulling away from the house we'd been renting for the last couple years brought tears to my eyes. Not because I was sad, but because it was finally over. It had felt like it would never end. Everything kept piling up more and more. Like I would never be able to breathe again.

It has started with three years of hospital visits to the point where everyone including Gray had nearly convinced me I was crazy.

To the final diagnosis—multiple sclerosis.

Not a death sentence. But a lifelong autoimmune disorder that explained every one of the problems I'd been having along the way. Then I'd spent the last year working to get it under control.

Just in time daddy to die, Gray to steal the money, and the divorce.

Now I could start over.

I inhaled deeply and left without looking back.

By the time I got home, I was all cried out. No more tears for the life I left behind with my high school sweetheart.

Only looking forward to the new one I was determined to live on the ranch I'd always called home.

My heart clenched at the site before me—Rivers' Ranch. I'd missed the flat land, the oil rigs, the wide, wide open spaces. Midland-Odessa was a small piece of hell on earth, but it was home. My West Texas blood sang with remembrance. This was where I belonged.

My best friend's BMW was parked in the driveway when I pulled my truck and U-Haul up to the house. I shook my head as Tempi came into view, leaning back against the black car with her arms across her chest. The West Texas dust kicked up all around her and she just strode forward like the pageant queen she was.

I kicked the driver's side door open and dropped down unsteadily. "What the fuck are you doing here?"

"Had to show up for your big day back!"

Tempi threw her arms around me, squeezing me as tight as humanly possible. I gasped and patted her back.

"Thanks, Temp. But how did you know I'd be here?"

"You shared your location with me like four years ago when we went on that trip to Cabo, remember?"

I guffawed. "And you've kept it on ever since?"

"Obviously. A girl has to be safe."

"I love you." I shook my head and squeezed her harder.

"Of course you do. I'm easy to love."

She was. I'd known Temperance Baldwin since I was six years old. We'd been in the same dance class, which I'd promptly flunked out of, if it was possible to fail ballet. She'd gone on to be good enough to dance on pointe for all the pageants that paid for all four years of college. Her long hair so dark it was nearly black and eyes so dark, they shined like onyx. She was tall and lithe with a Crest commercial smile and flawless make-up. She was also the complete opposite of her namesake. She had never done a single thing in moderation.

We couldn't have been more disparate and yet, we'd worked. Both loners who had found each other. The pageant queen and the cowgirl. And it had stuck.

"So why are you stalking me?" I asked as I followed her toward the ranch house.

We climbed the few stairs and I unlocked the door. The screen door clattered behind us as we stepped into my daddy's house. I breathed in the scent of my childhood home. It was a one story that had been in the family for generations. It had been added on sometimes haphazardly until it had sprawled beyond its scope with winding rooms and strange quirks. I loved all of them.

"When your best friend moves home, you celebrate." She reached into her giant purse and removed a bottle of whiskey.

I laughed. "It's the middle of the afternoon."

"Yeah, so I thought we could pregame," she said, following me into the living room where I set down my own tiny purse and pocketed my phone.

"Pregame...for what?" I asked cautiously.

It was always something with Tempi. I'd had a very long day and all I wanted to do was take a nap. I couldn't even think about unloading the truck. Shawn, who ran the ranch in my father's stead, said he would help once he was off for the day. So I had planned to leave it in the drive and pass out in my old bedroom in the meantime.

"So, there's a charity ball."

"No." I stepped around her. "You know that I'm so out of place at those things."

"You are not. It'll be fun."

I shot her a disbelieving look. "You always say that and it's never fun."

"This one is different."

"Why?"

"Because you're single!"

I shuddered at that word. I was divorced, but I hadn't said the word single out loud yet. As terrible as my relationship with Grayson had ended, it had been *perfect* before that point. At fourteen years old, I'd stepped into my advanced geometry class and found the boy of my dreams. We'd dated for seven years where neither of us once looked at anyone else. We were engaged my senior year and married the weekend after graduation. Three weeks later we were in an apartment in Denver as he started his own marketing firm and I wrangled horses at a nearby park. I'd hated leaving home, but life was too good.

Until it wasn't.

And I was *not* ready to face the fact that my marriage had fallen apart so thoroughly when I was the only person in my friend group who had always had it together.

"Let's not."

Tempi sighed. "I knew you'd be like this. So don't worry. I brought back up supplies."

"Do I want to know what that means?"

Tempi disappeared back through the front door and was back a minute later with a long black bag.

"Oh no," I whispered.

"I brought something for you to wear."

"Temp..."

"You'll be my plus one."

"It's day *one*," I groaned.

Tempi wasn't having any of it. After she helped me bring in my suitcase and unpack a *singular* box, she had me in the primary bedroom, fixing my hair and make-up. Something I'd learned long ago was to never underestimate Tempi. She might look like prom queen Cordelia Chase, but she had Willow's brains and Buffy's determination.

At least there was whiskey.

"So, who are you dating now?" I asked.

She shrugged. "No one."

"Is that code for there are too many and you forgot their names?"

"Maybe," she teased.

I arched an eyebrow.

"Okay, Dane might be going to the event tonight, and I'm very interested in leaving with him."

"There it is," I said with a laugh.

"I hate you," Tempi said as she finished up my hair.

"You love me."

"So fucking hard, bitch. Now let's get you into this gown and heels."

I grimaced. I couldn't walk in heels on a good day.

With my added balance issues from my illness, I wasn't sure I would ever want to be back in them.

"You know I walk like a baby giraffe in those things."

Tempi saw my look and softened. "They're chunky heel and I added these inserts to them so they'll be easier to manage."

I removed the slinky silky dress, pulling it over my frame. The material was like water poured over my skin. And thanks to the fact that Tempi had stayed in pageant shape and I'd been in and out of the hospital a lot, we were no longer *exactly* the same size. My hips strained against the material and my boobs...holy fuck, my boobs. They practically sprung out of the sage green dress.

I slipped my feet into the heels. To her credit they were more comfortable, but I was still unsteady as I came back into view.

"Fuck me," Tempi said, fanning herself. "You're going to get every guy in the place looking at you."

"You know I'm not interested, right?"

"Look you've had the same dick since you were fourteen, it's time to branch out." Tempi poured another knuckles worth of whiskey and passed it to me.

"I'd rather not."

She held her glass up to mine and we clinked as she declared, "Sample platter!"

I laughed and tipped the drink back. I probably shouldn't get drunk on my meds, but Tempi was fucking contagious.

"We're going to have the best time," Tempi said. "Forget all about what's-his-name and let's find you someone to go home with."

I shook my head at my best friend. I had no intention of going home with *anyone*. But it was nice to do something other than wallow in my grief over the loss of my father, husband, and autonomy for once.

Today, I was just a woman in a killer dress.

Time to live a little.

ACKNOWLEDGMENTS

Ahhh! This isn't just the conclusion to Chase & Harley's story, but the conclusion to the Wrights. I never ever in a million years thought this series would become as long as it did. I actually wasn't sure I'd even write a second book. Now I'm here at book FIFTEEN!

I couldn't have done any of this without the support of all of my readers. Anyone who picked up any of my books. The millions of people who have read the Wrights in all their various iterations. Thank you so much. And who knows...maybe this isn't a forever closing of the door!

The soundtrack to this book was: 1989 vault tracks from Taylor Swift especially Is It Over Now?, also Daylight (because they're golden!), What Do You Make of Me by Beth Crowley, What Was I Made For? by Billie Eilish, The Nest by Sody, and Sweet Creature by Harry Styles.

ABOUT THE AUTHOR

K.A. Linde is the *USA Today* bestselling author of more than thirty novels. She has a Masters degree in political science from the University of Georgia and served as the head coach of the Duke University dance team. She loves reading fantasy novels, binge-watching Buffy, traveling to far off destinations, baking insane desserts, and dancing in her spare time.

She currently lives in Lubbock, Texas, with her husband, son, and super adorable puppy.

Visit her online:

www.kalinde.com

Or Facebook, Instagram & Tiktok:
@authorkalinde

For exclusive content, free books,
and giveaways every month.
www.kalinde.com/subscribe